BREAKWATER PROTECTOR

SALTWATER COWBOYS, BOOK 2

CHRISTY BARRITT

River Heights

CHAPTER ONE

"PRESTON!" Lizzie McCreary pushed through the thick trees and blinked into the blackness surrounding her.

Clouds covered the full moon, leaving her shrouded in darkness.

She had to find her son. He was in this gnarled, sandy wilderness all alone.

Her heart lurched into her throat at the thought.

Copperheads and water moccasins were common out here. So were wild boar. Sometimes even bears. Lizzie had read about them in a brochure left at her rental house.

Panic seized her at the taunting images . . . especially when mixed with the thought of her missing eight-year-old.

"Preston!" Her throat ached from yelling his name.

But she wasn't going to stop.

Not until she found her son.

Lizzie paused next to a live oak and sucked in a ragged breath. She needed to gather her thoughts. To think logically.

As she blew the air from her lungs only to inhale again, the scent of dead leaves and salty ocean air drifted around her. Dry grass tangled around her legs. Somewhere in the distance, an animal howled.

She shivered.

Where could Preston be? There were so many crevices, so many trees, so many places a boy could hide in these woods.

She had to find him. He was the only person Lizzie had left in this world. If she lost him . . .

A cry escaped her throat. She couldn't bear the thought of it.

Preston was the reason she got up every morning. The bright spot in her days, especially after everything that had happened . . .

Lizzie glanced at her phone and frowned. She still had no signal, still couldn't call for help.

What was she going to do?

"Preston!" She staggered away from the tree.

Panic made her head swirl, made her steps unsteady.

She stumbled forward anyway. She would search these woods all evening and all night if she had to.

As she took another step, her leg plunged into water—all the way to her knee.

Lizzie sucked in a breath.

She'd stepped into some type of watery crevice, a swampy pothole of sorts. Gloppy sand at the bottom of the puddle gripped her left leg.

She tried to wrench herself out, but the residue suctioned her leg in place.

Lizzie tugged again, but the motion only seemed to make the sand tighten around her calf.

Another round of panic hit her.

No, no, no!

Lizzie had to find her son. She didn't have time for this. Why was it so difficult to get her leg out of this sand pit?

As she tugged again, a noise in the distance caught her ear.

Her head swerved up, and she strained to see through the darkness.

"Mom?" a small voice asked.

"Preston?" *Please Lord, don't let me be imagining things. Let that be him.*

Someone stepped from the shadows, the moonlight illuminating his figure.

"Preston! It's me. Mom. I'm here." Relief washed through Lizzie, followed by another wave of concern.

"I can't see you." His voice—normally gregarious —sounded thin with fear.

"I'm going to come get you, honey." Lizzie tugged her leg again. It was still stuck in the sediment beneath the water.

What was this? Quicksand? That was just a Hollywood myth, right? Or did it really exist in coastal North Carolina?

Lizzie lowered herself to the ground and yanked her leg again, desperate to remove herself from the waterlogged sand.

It didn't matter what she did, though.

Her leg wouldn't budge. The good news was that it wasn't pulling her under, as portrayed in the movies.

"Mom?" Preston's voice stretched through the darkness.

She looked back at him as he stood near a tree across the opening. An empty space—probably twenty feet—stretched between them.

He was so close yet so far away.

Something rustled in the brush on the other side of the open area.

Lizzie sucked in a breath at the sound. What was that?

Before the question could fully form in her mind, something emerged from the foliage.

A boar.

The creature stared at Preston, ready to charge.

DASH FULTON PAUSED on his horse as he heard a commotion in the distance. Were the wild horses fighting nearby? He supposed it could be a scuffle between mares or that one of the foals might be injured.

Whatever it was, danger crackled through the autumn air like an approaching storm.

He nudged his horse, Shadrach, to go faster as they headed toward a region of the island known as Wash Woods.

Too many dangers lurked in the wild there.

Especially at this time of night.

Another sound caught his ear, and tension threaded across his muscles. Was that a yell?

What if it wasn't a horse in trouble but a person?

As a law enforcement officer, Dash patrolled the island tonight, on the lookout for any trouble. Normally, he remained beachside so he could monitor the wild horses and make sure no one was trying to feed or ride them. But tonight, he'd cut over the dune and wandered toward the woods on the other side of Cape Corral.

The decision appeared to be serendipitous.

As clear as day, he heard a woman shout, "Preston!"

What was going on out here? Dash needed to find out before somebody got hurt.

He prodded his horse, and Shadrach began to gallop as they headed toward the area, following the voice. But this island contained eight thousand acres, and at least a thousand of those were Wash Woods. Finding someone in the dense, tangled forest would be difficult.

Lord, guide me.

Finally, Dash reached the edge of the thick brush that grew on the west side of the island. Fitting between the foliage was always a challenge. Live oaks, wax myrtles, and pines intertwined with each other, their branches forming a fortress that silently defied anyone to dare enter.

The area had once been sand dunes, but Mother

Nature had a change of heart. In recent decades, a forest had sprouted on the hills. Something about the area had always felt a bit enchanted and creepy.

Cape Corral was generally flat, a sandbar-like island. But in Wash Woods, the atmosphere and environment made you feel as if you'd disappeared into the hollows of West Virginia. The hills weren't as big, but they were still there, along with creeks filled with black water.

Unlike West Virginia, moss hung from the trees. Black, tarlike puddles pooled in low-lying areas—puddles laden with snakes and leeches and other critters most people didn't want to encounter.

"Preston, stop!"

Dash heard the voice again. What were people doing out here at this time of night? Had some college kids decided to camp in the area again? It happened a few times every year. The thrill-seeking teens didn't realize the danger they put themselves in.

Whatever was happening, it didn't sound good.

He ducked as more low branches stretched in his path. The trail was becoming narrower and narrower by the moment. Soon, the trees would be so thick that Dash would have to get off his horse and go on foot. He hoped that didn't happen.

Even though Dash officially worked as a law enforcement officer for the Forestry Division, unofficially he was known as a saltwater cowboy.

He knew enough to know there are some places that no one should walk at night.

These woods were one of them.

He pulled a flashlight from his belt and shone it around him.

That's when he caught sight of what was happening.

A boy, probably eight years old, stood against the edge of the forest.

Even in the moonlight, Dash saw the child's wide, terrified eyes.

Dash jerked his gaze in the other direction. A woman sprawled on the ground, clawing at the sand. Had her leg gotten caught in an animal trap?

The Jezebel Tree hovered above her. The gnarled live oak was legendary in the area.

A grunt filled the air, and Dash swerved his flashlight toward the noise.

Just across the open expanse, a wild boar snarled.

Dash's heart lurched into his throat.

A wild boar?

Dash didn't have much time to make his move.

The air cracked with danger, and the night was about to turn ugly.

"Come on, let's go!" He nudged Shadrach.

They galloped across the opening in the woods. As they did, the boar, with its sharp tusks protruding from its snout, charged toward the boy.

He couldn't let that animal get to the boy before he did. The child would never survive the collision.

Dash's stomach clenched tighter as the boy cried out in fear. The child appeared frozen in place.

Dash clucked his tongue. "Faster, Shad. Faster!"

The boy screamed but still didn't move.

Just a few more feet, Dash told himself. A few more feet, and he could help the boy.

His lungs tightened as he got closer.

Dear Lord . . . help him. Help me help him.

Behind him, the woman's scream was garbled with fear.

Two feet.

Two feet and that boar would get the boy.

Not on Dash's watch.

Three seconds later, Dash reached down. As Shadrach galloped past, Dash scooped the boy up with one arm. His stallion continued bolting across the sand until the expanse ended.

Then Shadrach snorted and rose up on his hind

legs as a wall of trees appeared in front of him. Back on all four, the horse paced and turned.

Dash glanced back just in time to see the boar collide with the tree. The creature stiffened, appearing dazed, until finally it scampered back into the woods.

Dash let out his breath and held the boy to his chest.

That could have turned out so much differently.

Praise God it hadn't.

"Are you okay?" He quickly scanned the boy.

The child clung to Dash as if his life depended on it. He said nothing, only cried quietly into Dash's chest.

From Dash's quick perusal, he didn't see any injuries. Hopefully, the boy's scars would just be emotional. Those could be equally as scary, but, since medical care was sparse on the island, it was still the best of the options.

Now Dash needed to get to the boy's mom. He didn't have any time to waste.

That boar could come back any minute—and if it returned, it could be with a vengeance.

CHAPTER TWO

LIZZIE NEARLY COLLAPSED with relief when she realized Preston was safe. The boar was gone. And a handsome rescuer had swept onto the scene just in time.

In other circumstances, Lizzie might wonder where the cowboy had come from. Right now, she didn't care. She was just thankful that this man had literally ridden in like a knight in shining armor to save the day.

The cowboy stopped beside her and climbed from the horse. He helped Preston down, and her son rushed into her arms.

"Mom, Mom! I was so scared!"

Lizzie hugged Preston close, vowing to never let

him go—though she knew she couldn't do that. The boy was growing up entirely too fast.

"I was so worried about you," she murmured into his sweaty brown hair. His boyish scent filled her with comfort—and gratitude.

She'd thought she was going to lose him. She swallowed a cry at the thought.

Her gaze flickered up to the cowboy who stood near his horse.

"Thank you." Her voice cracked.

"It's no problem, ma'am." The man tilted his hat at her before glancing around. "But we need to get you two out of here before that boar comes back."

Lizzie tensed at the idea of seeing that creature again. She'd never realized just how dangerous they could be.

"I'm . . ." She tugged at her leg again, hoping for a different outcome than when she'd tried moments earlier. No such luck. "I'm . . . stuck."

The man kneeled in front of her and pointed at her leg, as if asking permission to touch her. "Do you mind?"

A cowboy *and* a gentleman? What kind of place had she come to? Lizzie wasn't complaining.

"Whatever you need to do." Lizzie would say yes

to dancing with a tornado right now if it meant getting her and Preston out of here.

He gripped her calf and tugged.

Nothing happened.

After trying again, the man grunted and straightened. His gaze remained on the water-saturated sand that acted as her shackle and chain as it suctioned her in place.

"Is it quicksand?" Lizzie rushed.

The man stared at the spot. "It could be. Believe it or not, we do have some of that around here."

More panic seized her muscles. "Am I going to be stuck here?"

"Not forever. I'll dig you out."

Would he have to leave to get a shovel? Lizzie's lungs tightened at the thought of being out here alone. She craved the safety of her rental house. She'd come here to disappear. To feel invisible.

So far, her plan hadn't fleshed out.

"But . . ." She tried to think of an alternative to having her hero leave her in this dark wilderness.

The man's gaze flickered to her, and he seemed to read the panic in her eyes. "I'll use my hands."

Relief washed through Lizzie. "Oh . . . okay."

On his knees, the man began sludging wet sand

from around her leg. "As I work, see if you can pull up your leg, okay?"

"Of course." Lizzie held Preston tighter. Her son still hugged her, the tightness of his embrace indicating he didn't want to let go either.

As she felt some of the suction disappearing from around her leg, she pulled again. But she still couldn't get herself free. She'd never experienced anything like this before. Had never been nature's prisoner.

She fought the tears that wanted to rush to her eyes.

Something rustled in the brush in the distance, and Lizzie's lungs froze. The cowboy seemed to hear the sound too. He glanced over his shoulder and began to dig faster.

Preston released her as she squirmed, desperate to get out of these woods.

"Give it another tug," the man instructed, his voice still calm and absent of any panic.

Lizzie rose on one knee and pulled again. This time, she flew backward. The man caught her before she toppled onto the ground.

Her loafer was gone, leaving her foot bare, but her leg was free.

She was free.

Praise God!

She shook her leg, trying to get the wet sand off as gratitude and relief filled her. She glanced at the man who'd been such a lifesaver tonight. "Thank you. Thank you so much."

The cowboy glanced back as more rustling sounded in the brush. "We need to get you back to safety. Are you staying far from here?"

"Not too far. Over on Sandfiddler Court."

With one last glance at the rustling, the cowboy nodded. "Come on. I'll give you a ride."

"You don't have to—"

"Yes, I do. Now, come on. We don't have time to argue."

Without asking any more questions, he helped Lizzie mount the horse before assisting Preston to his spot in front of her. Lizzie positioned her arms on both sides of her son as she grabbed the saddle horn and held on. The cowboy took the reins and led them through the woods.

Lizzie thanked God for her guardian angel tonight.

But she knew they weren't out of danger yet.

So she would keep praying.

DASH REMAINED on guard as he led Shadrach through the dense forest.

He'd heard the rustling in the woods. He knew the boar could appear again at any minute. The faster he could get these two out of here, the better.

But as he glanced up at the woman and her son, he saw the tension on their faces. They were traumatized and afraid, as anyone in their situation would be. He was just relieved he'd gotten here when he did.

"So, what are your names?" Dash needed to distract them.

"Am I allowed to tell him, Mom?" The boy looked up at his mom with wide, questioning eyes.

"Yes, sweetie. Go ahead."

"I'm Preston."

"Nice to meet you, Preston. My name is Dash."

"Dash? I've never met anybody named Dash. But there's a boy named Dash in my favorite movie."

"*The Incredibles*?"

The boy grinned. "Have you seen it?"

"I actually have. I watched it with my cousin's kids."

"Isn't it the best?"

"Definitely." Dash glanced at Preston. "Are you fast like the boy in the movie?"

"I like to pretend I am," Preston said. "But I'm not really. Maybe when I get older. My mom says I'm more of the strong type, like a linebacker instead of a running back."

"There's nothing wrong with that." Dash glanced up at the woman, waiting to hear if she'd say anything.

"And I'm Lizzie, Preston's mom. Thank you for saving us back there."

Dash didn't tell her that they weren't out of the woods yet, figuratively or literally. Certainly, she knew that and didn't need to hear it reiterated.

"It's no problem," Dash said. "I'm glad I was close."

"So are we. Otherwise . . ." The woman shuddered and didn't finish her sentence.

They both knew what the outcome would have been—Preston had come only inches from being gored, all while Lizzie was stuck, only to helplessly watch. The thought of it caused a sick feeling to gurgle in his stomach.

"It's late to be out here roaming these woods," Dash said. "Actually, I don't recommend roaming them during the day either."

"Preston and I are going to have a little talk about that later," Lizzie said. "Aren't we, Preston?"

"I just wanted to see what was out here. I thought I saw a horse, and I wanted to see where it was going."

"Why would you do that, sweetie?" Tension laced the woman's words. "You know better."

"I like horses."

"You shouldn't be running off at night without asking me," Lizzie said. "You scared me to death."

The boy frowned as they sauntered along. "I'm sorry."

Just ahead, Dash spotted the clearing in the woods. Not much farther, and they should be at the house where these two were staying. He hoped. Not many houses were on that lane, making it one of the more secluded areas on the island.

But, in reality, the whole island was secluded.

Something about the woman's tension and the boy's curiosity had Dash on edge.

He sensed there was more to their story than they let on.

And he was curious to know what.

CHAPTER THREE

RELIEF FILLED Lizzie as soon as she spotted the rental house nestled between the dunes in the distance. Safety was officially in sight. Some of the lights had been left on, which made the place look more welcoming.

She pointed to the structure. "Right there."

"Roger that."

Dash led the horse to the two-story cottage and tied his reins on one of the posts beneath the house. The structure was stilted, like many in the area. Though it was Lizzie's first time on the island, she knew the buildings were constructed like this in case a storm surge swept through the island. The place made her feel like she was living in a giant treehouse.

"Let me help you down." Dash reached for Preston.

Preston swung his leg over the side of the horse and slid into Dash's arms. After Dash deposited the boy on the sand, he reached for Lizzie.

She tried to effortlessly slide down like Preston. But instead she stumbled and nearly fell into Dash.

She clutched his shirt as she caught herself.

Just as quickly, Lizzie realized what she'd done and stepped back, absently straightening herself and smoothing her shirt.

"Sorry about that," she muttered.

"It's no problem." Dash appeared to fight a smile.

She pointed to the stairs in the distance that led to the front door. "We should get inside. I can't say thank you enough."

"I'd feel better if I checked out your leg before I left. There are sticks and all kinds of critters in that water. Leeches too. Would you mind?"

Lizzie didn't really want to invite a man into her house. But this one had just saved her life. Her gaze wandered to his belt. In the glow of her houselights, she could barely make out the badge there. As she suspected, he was some type of law enforcement in this area.

"Come on, Mom," Preston said. "I can introduce him to Gremlin."

Dash's eyebrows rose. "Gremlin?"

"He's my turtle. Mom let me bring him with me."

"I see." Dash's voice held a hint of amusement.

"I guess it couldn't hurt if you checked out my leg." The thought of having any blood-sucking critters attached to her made her feel woozy.

Lizzie was many things but not an outdoorswoman. And if a leech was attached to her?

She shuddered.

She had no idea what she would do.

She ignored the tremble that raked through her as she pulled off her remaining loafer and climbed the steps to her house. Preston walked beside her, with Dash following behind. At the top, she punched a code into the number pad before opening the front door. Her welcoming little cottage stared back at them.

Dash held the screen door as Lizzie stepped inside followed by Preston.

"Why don't you sit down?" Dash nodded toward the couch. "It should only take a moment to check you out."

Lizzie nodded, still feeling unreasonably nervous. But she sat on the teal-colored sofa and turned on another light beside her. As she did, Preston hurried into the kitchen and grabbed a juice box.

"Only one!" she called. "It's getting late."

"I know, Mom."

He was such a happy little boy. At least, he had been. The past few months had been hard on both of them. Lizzie prayed that coming here would be a nice change.

Dash knelt in front of her and tilted his cowboy hat back farther on his head. In the light, Lizzie got a better look at him.

She noted his square jaw. The slight prickle of hair across his cheeks and upper lip. When he glanced up, Lizzie caught sight of blue eyes.

Dash certainly was handsome. His cowboy boots, jeans, and plaid shirt only made him more of a mystery.

When she'd come to the barrier island off North Carolina's coast, she hadn't expected to feel like she'd stepped onto a Texas ranch. She'd been prepared for lifeguards and fishermen—not strapping cowboys on horseback.

Dash carefully examined her mud-covered legs. A scratch stretched on her left calf, but nothing that couldn't be fixed with some Neosporin and Band-Aids. Otherwise, she appeared okay.

"Are you a . . . paramedic?" she finally asked.

Dash let out a quick chuckle. "I suppose I didn't tell you what I did. Sorry about that. I'm Dash Fulton, one of the wildlife and law enforcement officers here on the island. We serve double duty. We not only look after the people, but we look after the wild horses as well."

Lizzie was already fascinated. She never imagined such a thing when she came here. Then again, she hadn't given much thought to where she was going. She'd only known that she had to leave and go off grid.

"I brought you a juice." Preston appeared beside Dash with a Capri Sun in his hands.

"Honey, Officer Fulton probably doesn't want any juice."

Dash winked at the boy. "Actually, they're my favorite. If you set it on the table, I'll grab it in a minute."

Preston's face lit with a grin, and he nodded, doing just as Dash said.

"I don't see any little critters on you." Dash straightened and offered a quick nod at Lizzie. "We just need to clean up that cut, and I think you'll be good to go."

Relief filled her yet again. Thank goodness there were no leeches. Even the thought of them made her skin crawl.

"Thank you," she murmured. "The rest of my ailments aren't anything that a nice shower won't fix."

"If you'd like, you can go get cleaned up, and I'll wait here with Preston."

The idea was intriguing, especially since she didn't want to leave her son alone right now—not after everything that happened. But was it a good idea?

Probably not.

"You don't have to do that," she finally told Dash. "You've already done so much."

"Ma'am, I'm on duty all night. I really don't mind. Besides, you're probably going to wait until he falls asleep before you shower, which means that you're going to be walking around with swamp goo on you for another couple of hours. Your boy is pretty wired. I think it would do you a world of good just to get cleaned up. But don't mind me. It's really none of my business."

She'd halfway expected to hear a country twang

to his voice. But she didn't. Instead, his voice sounded surprisingly cultured.

And that wasn't to mention his plan, which sounded divine. Lizzie wanted to argue that it didn't. She wanted to say she didn't trust him. But neither of those things were true.

Something about this man beckoned her interest. Was it his badge? His heroic rescue?

She didn't know.

But maybe she should consider his offer.

Lizzie swept a hair behind her ear and nodded. "If you don't mind, I think I will clean up real fast. I'll only be a few minutes. If you could just keep an eye on the place." Her unspoken words lingered in the air.

But the message was clear: Lizzie needed Dash to make sure that Preston didn't wander outside again.

He'd taken to exploring by himself on more than one occasion lately. Lizzie had hoped and prayed he wouldn't do it here.

It had happened anyway—and when she'd been least expecting it. She'd asked Preston to get ready for bed while she did a video conference call for work. In the middle of her discussion, she'd realized she hadn't heard anything from her son in several minutes.

That's when she'd known something was wrong.

She'd followed Preston's footsteps in the sand to the nearby woods, realizing what he'd done.

"Absolutely," Dash said. "I'm going to sit down, enjoy my Capri Sun, and meet Gremlin."

"Can I show you my superhero figures too?" Preston's voice lit with excitement. Her son defined extroverted. He absolutely loved people and talking.

"I'd love to see them."

With one more reluctant glance, Lizzie escaped upstairs to her shower. She would make this as quick as possible . . . because she wasn't in the habit of leaving her son with strangers.

For that matter, she really didn't leave her son with anyone.

Especially after everything that had happened.

"I DIDN'T WANT to come to this place," Preston said.

Dash glanced at the boy as he held the box turtle, carefully flying him like a superhero through the air. "Is that right? But Cape Corral is a nice place."

"So is my house. But mom said we had to go, and

we had to go quickly. I hardly had time to even get Gremlin."

Dash's curiosity spiked. Why had this woman and her son had to leave so fast? Something about the statement didn't sit well with him. Were the two of them in trouble?

Dash sipped his drink until the straw rattled and gurgled as the pouch emptied of its juice. "How long will you be here?"

Preston placed the turtle back into his terrarium and shrugged. "I'm not sure. Maybe forever."

Dash's eyebrows flickered up. "I see. At least you have your turtle with you."

"That's right." Preston nodded. "He always makes everything better. Mom said maybe we can get a dog if we stay here for a while. I love animals."

"So I heard. But you shouldn't be wandering around outside by yourself, understand? Things could have turned out very badly tonight."

Preston frowned and ran his finger down his turtle's shell. "I know. I'm sorry. I just wanted to see what was out there."

"That can be very dangerous," Dash told him. "There are not only boars out there. People have spotted an occasional bear, along with foxes and some pretty dangerous snakes."

Preston's eyes widened. "Snakes? I love snakes."

Nothing got this boy down, did it? "You wouldn't like these snakes. Believe me. One of them bit one of our horses, and we almost lost her because of it. Her name is KitKat."

His eyes widened even more. "Wow. I like her name."

Dash nodded. "Wow is right. It was scary."

Footsteps pounded down the stairs, and Lizzie appeared at the base of the steps. He sucked in a breath at the sight of her.

The woman had long, dark hair that hung straight and silky. Olive skin. Even features. A slim build. Between her height and looks, she could have probably been a model if she had wanted.

No doubt about it—she was beautiful. Dash couldn't help but wonder exactly what her story was.

And there was also the fact that Preston looked nothing like her. The boy had blond hair, a stocky build, and blue eyes.

That didn't mean anything. Dash knew children didn't always resemble their mom or dad. Maybe Preston looked just like his father.

But that didn't stop the questions from racing through Dash's mind.

"I see that you met Gremlin." Lizzie paused near them and glanced down at the turtle.

As she did, Dash rose to his feet. "You've got one very curious boy with a lot of personality."

She smiled, pride beaming from her gaze. "No truer statement has ever been spoken."

Just as the words left her mouth, a noise sounded outside.

In an instant, Lizzie's face went as white as a ghost.

She stepped toward her son, appearing ready to either run or fight.

Then her gaze met Dash's.

Her voice trembled as she asked, "What was that?"

CHAPTER FOUR

LIZZIE LINGERED IN THE KITCHEN, Preston huddled beside her, as she waited for Dash to return from checking things outside.

Thank goodness, the man had been here. Lizzie didn't know what that noise was. But she'd heard something.

Maybe even a person. Someone dangerous.

Someone who'd followed her here.

Her heart beat furiously against her chest at the thought.

As steps pounded up the outdoor stairs, Lizzie held her breath.

A moment later, the door handle twisted.

She pulled Preston tighter against her. Her gaze darted toward the kitchen counter where some knives sat in a butcher block. She should have grabbed one. Maybe she should have bought a gun before she came here. Only she hadn't had time. Everything had happened so fast.

As the door opened, she could hardly breathe. Worst-case scenarios flashed through her mind.

Until . . . Dash stepped inside.

She released the air from her lungs, but the tension across her chest remained.

"Something spooked Shadrach," he explained.

Lizzie nodded. She supposed that made sense. But it didn't necessarily make her feel any better. "Any idea what?"

"Could have been a wild animal. Maybe a snake." Dash shrugged. "Hard to say."

"You didn't see . . . anything else out there?" She'd tried not to let fear capture her voice, but it hadn't worked. Her words sounded too raw, too unsteady.

"I didn't see anything." Dash's cowboy boots clunked across the wood floor as he came closer. "It's not like Shadrach to get upset, but as I said, if he saw a snake, there's no way he'd just stand by calmly."

"I'm glad he's okay."

Dash studied Lizzie's face for one more minute, as if trying to read her reaction.

Instantly, Lizzie tried to put up the walls she'd spent so much time constructing—walls that kept her private life private. But her eyes often gave her away. That's what her mom had always told her.

"Me too," Dash finally said before nodding behind him. "I guess I should get going. I'll let the two of you get some rest."

Lizzie halfway wished the man would stay longer. But that thought was ridiculous. Lizzie didn't even know him. Besides, he'd done his duty as a law enforcement officer. There was no reason for him to stay any longer.

She cleared her throat. "I can't say thank you enough for everything you did tonight. You saved my son and me. Thank you again."

Dash tipped his hat. "It's no problem. I'll leave my number in case you need anything else. Otherwise, I hope you enjoy your stay here in Cape Corral."

AS DASH RODE AWAY from the house, his mind remained on the woman and her son.

Lizzie was definitely jumpy. Jumpier than most people he'd met.

Dash's gut told him she was in trouble. It was the only thing that made sense. When he put together what Preston had said about them coming here quickly, combined with the woman's edginess, his theory seemed plausible.

That worried him.

Lizzie had picked a house that was relatively isolated here on the island. It didn't appear that anyone else was staying in either of the other two houses closest to her.

Tourist season was over, and most of the people who came to this area in October were fishermen who preferred to stay near the water. Lizzie's rental was in the middle of the island, within walking distance of the notorious Wash Woods.

Dash would need to keep an eye on Lizzie and Preston while they were here—at least until he figured out what was going on. He'd do it out of an abundance of caution.

He nudged Shadrach as they cantered into the darkness. Dash needed to get back to headquarters and put his horse in the stable for the night.

But his mind wouldn't leave the woman and her son.

Was it because they reminded Dash so much of himself and his mom when he'd been growing up?

For so long, it had been just the two of them. Dash clearly remembered their struggles.

It was hard to say what exactly drew his attention. But something about the mother-son duo made his thoughts spin.

If Dash was smart, he'd put them out of his mind. He had enough to worry about right now. *More* than enough to worry about.

The tension between rich newcomers and long-time locals on the island was growing, and Dash knew he'd have to come clean with his friends soon about his role in what was happening behind the scenes.

He'd been withholding secrets from the community for entirely too long. But people were bound to find out any time now. It would be better if they heard it from Dash rather than someone else.

Yet he dreaded revealing the truth.

Because Dash dreaded how the truth would change things.

CHAPTER FIVE

THE MAN HUNKERED behind some sea oats on the sand dune and watched the cowboy on his horse as he trotted into the darkness.

Who did that man think he was? Involving himself in the lives of Lizzie and Preston? That wasn't that man's job.

It was *his* job. Nobody else was going to try and do it.

He crouched lower, just to make sure nobody saw him.

He'd thought about making his presence known. Thought about letting Lizzie know that she wasn't as smart as she thought. Thought about storming into the house and claiming what was his.

But he wouldn't do that. He needed time. Time

to come up with his plan. Time to figure out how to teach Lizzie a lesson.

She couldn't leave. He would always be a part of her life. The two of them were inexplicably intertwined.

That was why he'd followed her and Preston here.

Then he'd found the perfect hiding spot and he'd watched.

He'd watched the house. Watched as Preston snuck out.

He followed behind, waiting to see what would happen. The moonlight was just bright enough that he could make out some details.

He had even seen the boar. Seen Lizzie get stuck.

He'd almost stepped in to help. But he would have revealed his presence here if he did. It wasn't time yet.

So he'd hedged his bets.

He stared at the house again, at the lights glowing in the windows. The shades had been pulled, so he couldn't see what was happening inside. But he could imagine. He knew Lizzie well enough to know that she was probably stressed. She'd probably checked her locks more than once. She was probably on edge.

Good. She should be.

Because she should never have fled, should never have tried to hide.

How had Lizzie even known his intentions? He'd been so careful not to alarm her.

He fisted his hands as anger rushed through him.

Who did she think she was?

Soon, he'd put Lizzie in her place. It would be a lesson she'd never forget.

"You think you can lose me," he whispered. "But you can't. I'm here. I'm watching."

A thrill of delight sent a shiver through him as he imagined what the next few days might hold.

"You can't take what's mine," he muttered. "I'll figure out a way to get exactly what I want. You can count on it, Lizzie McCreary. Mark my words."

CHAPTER SIX

THE NEXT MORNING, Dash sat with his two coworkers at The Screen Porch Café.

It was the only restaurant on the island, and the name was just like it sounded. Mrs. Minnie Minnows and her husband, Mark, had set up an eating area at the back of their house. Every day, they served homemade food until their ingredients ran out.

On good days, the screens were open and the scent of the ocean floated inside, mingling with the savory aroma of fried bacon and fresh-baked bread. No matter what time of day, Old Bay still tinged the air, as well as crabmeat and garlic butter.

Dash, his boss, Levi Sutherland, and his coworker, Grant Matthews, liked to meet together for breakfast once a week. Their job was to protect the people of this island, as well as the horses.

"He was almost gored by a boar?" Grant repeated, his coffee cup raised in the air. "Right beside the Jezebel Tree? What in tarnation's going on here in Cape Corral? It's like this island wants more ghost stories to tell."

Dash shrugged and fought a smile. Grant loved antiquated expressions and words. He was the only twenty-something man Dash had ever met who used phrases like flabbergasted and catawampus.

"That boar was angry." Dash picked up a piece of his crisp bacon—as far as he was concerned, it was the only kind of bacon. None of that limp, half-cooked stuff would work. "I've never seen anything like it."

"What was the boy even doing out there at that time of night?" Levi asked.

"He thought he saw a horse and decided to follow." Dash raised his eyebrows and shrugged. "It's not the craziest story we've ever heard."

Grant clucked his tongue. "No, it's not."

Dash leaned back and tried to relax and pretend like this was an ordinary day. But in the back of his mind, he knew it was anything but ordinary.

Last night's events stayed with him. In fact, Dash

had replayed the scene over and over again when he should have been sleeping.

Preston had come so close to losing his life. The gleam of curiosity in the boy's eyes made Dash wonder if events like these were common. The thought didn't bring him any comfort.

"Did you say the woman got caught in quicksand?" Grant asked.

"That's right," Dash said. "I've never seen anything like it."

"I've only ever seen one other person get caught in quicksand here," Levi said. "It was probably ten years ago, and a man who was hunting in Wash Woods got stuck. We didn't find him for three days."

Grant's eyebrows shot up. "Did he survive?"

"He did. But I doubt he did any illegal hunting again."

Grant chuckled. "I guess not. Is it really quicksand?"

Levi nodded. "It is. Something about the water table here on the island makes it more susceptible to quicksand. Unlike in the movies, it won't pull you under. But it almost acts like wet cement. Once you're in, it's hard to get out."

Just as Dash picked up another piece of bacon and attempted to tune back into the conversation around him, his phone rang. When he glanced at the screen, he felt his face go pale and excused himself.

Stepping out of the restaurant, Dash paced far away from the open windows to make sure that nobody heard him.

"Hey, Clarkson." Dash jammed his free hand into his front jean pocket. "What's going on?"

"When are you going to tell people?" Clarkson's gruff voice cut to the heart of the matter.

Dash had figured that's what the man was calling about. But he'd hoped that maybe there was a different reason—a less abrasive one.

"I haven't figured it out yet," Dash finally said, gripping the phone a little too hard.

"I got more emails today here at the office. People are mad. Really mad. The situation would be cleared up if you just told people what you're doing."

Dash grimaced. "I'm not ready for that. I'm not ready for how the news will change people's perceptions of me."

"I worry that when people do find out, they won't forgive you—especially if this goes on for much longer. You should read some of these emails. People are threatening to sue. To ruin your life. And those are the nice messages."

His heart lurched. Dash knew how passionate people here on the island were. Though most of them didn't mean any harm, they also weren't afraid to fight for what they believed in.

"I'll figure it out," Dash said. "Soon. I promise."

"I hope so. Otherwise, I'm going to need a raise."

Dash held back his chuckle. "I'll be in touch."

He put his phone in his pocket and strode back inside the restaurant, trying to pretend like the conversation wasn't pressing on his mind.

But as Levi and Grant glanced at him, Dash had no doubt they noticed something different about him. That was the problem with having two friends who were in law enforcement. They were trained to pick up on subtle differences.

"Everything okay?" Levi stabbed another piece of his sausage as he observed Dash.

"Just fine." Dash took his seat at the table, his eggs and hash browns now cold. "Taking care of some business."

"I reckon you are," Grant muttered.

Dash quickly finished his coffee. Feeling desperate to avoid any more of this conversation, he rose. "I should run."

"Where are you heading?" Curiosity lingered in Levi's gaze.

Dash placed his hat back over his head. "I want to follow up with that mother and son I helped last night, to make sure they're okay."

"It sounds like it was quite the ordeal. I'm glad everything turned out okay."

Dash grimaced as an image flashed in his mind of that boar charging toward Preston. "I can't tell you how close that boy came to not making it."

"I hope everything goes well when you check on them," Levi said.

Dash remembered the uneasy look in Lizzie's eyes last night—a look that made it clear she was hiding something.

"Me too," Dash muttered. "Me too."

PRESTON STARED at his mom from across the table, his eyes on her instead of his schoolwork.

"What are we going to do today?" he repeated.

Lizzie looked up from her laptop and frowned. "I need you to complete those worksheets while I finish checking these invoices."

He exaggerated a frown. "Worksheets are boring. I want to go to the beach. I want to explore!"

"And we will do that soon enough. I promise. But

Mom's got to get some work done first. You know I already told you that."

"But—"

Before Preston could plead his case anymore, a knock sounded at the door.

Lizzie jumped to her feet. She pushed Preston behind her and stared at the front of the house. Her heart crashed into her chest.

Who could be here? No one knew her in Cape Corral, nor did anyone know she was coming here.

Her throat tightened as she swallowed hard. She couldn't ignore the person at the door. The truck she'd bought when she'd arrived was parked beneath the house. It would be obvious that she was home.

The knock sounded again, followed by a "Hello?"

Why did that voice sound vaguely familiar?

"It's Officer Fulton. Anybody home?"

Lizzie let out the breath she'd held. Dash? What was he doing here again?

It didn't matter.

She rushed to the door and pulled it open. Dash tipped his hat to her.

She sucked in a breath at the sight of him. Even though Lizzie had seen the man last night, she'd been tired and dirty. It had been late. And she'd been beside herself with worry over what had almost happened with Preston in the woods.

Seeing Dash as daylight washed over him caused her to pause. The man was even more handsome than she'd remembered, especially when the sun illuminated his cowboy hat and muscular figure.

"Officer." Lizzie rubbed her clammy hands on her jeans. Clammy hands? Why were her nerves acting up right now? She'd rationalize about that later. "I wasn't expecting to see you here."

"Can I come in?" He nodded toward her.

"Of course." She extended her hand toward the living room, suddenly wishing she'd taken more time to fix herself up. Oh, well. It didn't really matter. It wasn't like she was trying to impress anyone or looking for romance. Actually, she was nowhere close to looking for romance.

"Dash! Dash! Dash!" Preston ran across the room and threw his arms around Dash's waist.

Lizzie started to tell him to stop. Then she realized this man was probably her son's hero. All those shows Preston saw on TV where the good guys saved people in distress . . . and now a cowboy on horseback had saved him. Maybe the boy's hero complex wasn't a bad thing. Her son certainly needed something to look forward to and someone to look up to.

"Hey there, buddy." Dash patted his back. "Good to see you."

"Can I get you something to drink?" Lizzie asked. "Some coffee or water? Unfortunately, I don't have much to offer. I need to run to the store."

"No, that's okay. I don't want to overstay my welcome. I was doing my rounds this morning, and I thought I'd stop by to see how you're doing. I know last night was unnerving."

Lizzie's muscles loosened even more at his thoughtfulness. "We're fine this morning. Don't get me wrong, we won't forget what happened last night in those woods for a long time. But we're okay."

"I'm glad to hear that."

She nodded, unsure what to do with the flutter of nerves she felt. This wasn't her usual MO. Normally, she was known as an accomplished businesswoman and champion single mother. But right now, she felt like a fish out of water, as the saying went.

"Are you sure I can't get you something to drink?" she asked again. "Maybe some coffee?"

"Now that you mention it, maybe I will have some coffee. It's a little brisk outside this morning."

"Very well then. Have a seat."

Another rumble of nerves shimmied through

Lizzie as she walked into the kitchen. Thankfully, the space was open so she could still see Dash and Preston as she poured his coffee.

But Lizzie didn't need to make the man feel welcome here.

Preston had already led him to the couch and sat beside him.

Now, he was talking the man's ear off.

Lizzie fought a smile. Though she didn't want the boy to get too close, it was good to see him happy again. For a while, she hadn't been sure she'd ever see that again. As a mom, it had been hard to watch.

She poured the coffee and carried it out to Dash. Then she lowered herself into the chair across from him.

Dash started to thank her, but he could hardly get a word out as Preston kept talking about being a cowboy and telling him about the wild horses outside the house this morning.

"Can I go see your horse sometime?" Preston asked.

"Preston . . ." Warning strained Lizzie's voice. Preston did *not* need to be inviting himself out with this man.

"I would love for you to meet Shadrach again

sometime. And I can tell you a little about the wild horses here on the island."

"I want to watch them! But we just got here yesterday, and we haven't had time yet."

Dash glanced at Lizzie. "Is that right? Where are you from?"

Lizzie jumped in before her son shared something he shouldn't. "We're from a small town up near Maryland. Probably nowhere you've ever heard of."

"Maryland is nice."

"It is. But Cape Corral is a good change of pace."

Dash studied her a moment. Lizzie had probably answered too fast. She needed to slow her thoughts and head off her panic before she gave away something she shouldn't.

"You didn't have any more trouble around here last night, did you?" Dash asked.

"No, it was quiet." Lizzie didn't bother to tell him how she'd jumped at every noise and hardly gotten any sleep.

Evenings like last night weren't going to work for the long haul. She needed her rest if she was going to both work and homeschool. For so long, she'd been living in so much fear. Lizzie had to make some changes.

"It's usually quiet around here," Dash said. "This is the quietest season of all."

"Why do you say that?" Lizzie asked. "I would assume that winter was the quietest season."

"In the summer, all I hear is the hum of people's AC units. And in the winter, it's the same—except I hear the hum of heating units. Besides, my windows are closed then. But in the fall, I open my windows. When I listen closely, it's quiet enough that I can hear the ocean waves crashing in the distance."

Something about his description warmed Lizzie's heart and filled her imagination. But would she even be able to rest with her windows open? Even with the house being on stilts, which would make it nearly impossible to climb into from outside, she couldn't take any chances.

Dash took a few more sips of coffee before setting the cup back on the table and standing. "I should get going."

She glanced out the window. "By the way, where's your horse today? It looks like you drove your Bronco instead."

"I prefer patrolling the island on horseback. It's less intimidating for the wild horses. But there are times a vehicle is simply more practical."

"Makes sense."

Dash shifted. "I would love to take Preston to see the horses at our stable sometime."

Lizzie rose also. "Are you sure? Preston can be very excitable sometimes and—"

"No. I would love to. Really."

She couldn't think of any good excuse not to. "Okay then. That would be nice. Just let us know what time works for you."

"Can you meet me at the stable today at three?"

Could Lizzie be done with her work by then? She hoped so. She should be able to rearrange her schedule to make it work. There were a few perks to being her own boss.

"Please, Mom. Please, Mom. Please!" Preston made his puppy dog eyes . . . they always got to her.

"Okay, we can do it." She glanced back at Dash. "But if anything comes up or if it's inconvenient for you in any way, let us know."

Dash nodded. "I'll do that. You know how to get there?"

"No, but I can figure it out."

"Call me if you get lost. You two have a good day, and I'll see you in a few hours."

CHAPTER SEVEN

DASH LOOKED up as he heard somebody walk into the stable located behind the Community Safety building. The cedar-shingle-covered structure, which served as headquarters for the saltwater cowboys as well as the fire and rescue squad, was located in the center of the island.

Surprising pleasure filled Dash when he spotted Lizzie and Preston standing with the sunlight behind them, silhouetting their figures.

He placed his clipboard back into a locked box beside him. He'd just finished checking the medications for several horses. The fresh scent of hay and dirt rose around him, mixed with the leathery aroma of the saddles and riding gear.

He strode to greet his guests. "You made it. Good."

"This is awesome!" Preston's wide eyes scanned the stable.

The place was impressive with its wood-planked walls and high-beam ceiling. Sometimes in the morning when the sun rose, it lined perfectly with the arch atop the building, creating a movie-worthy atmosphere.

Lizzie kept her hand on her son's shoulder, probably trying to stop him from running ahead of her and doing something impulsive. "Thanks again for letting us come out. Preston has been so excited. I figured learning is learning, whether in the classroom or out in the real world."

"Couldn't agree more." Dash grinned and exchanged a look with her. "I'm glad you both can be here."

Lizzie's cheeks tinged a slight shade of pink before she pushed a lock of hair behind her ear. "Thanks for taking time from your day. I'm sure you're tired. Did you even get any sleep after last night?"

"I managed to grab a nap between my shifts." He winked. "Don't you worry about me."

"I just hate to impose."

"No imposing here." Dash turned to Preston. "Now, let me introduce you to some of these horses."

For the next hour, Dash told Preston about the horses. Eight were kept in the stable. These weren't wild horses from the island, but domesticated horses used to patrol the area.

Dash explained that it was important to keep the domesticated and wild horses apart so that disease didn't spread between them.

"What happens if one has to be treated?" Lizzie asked.

"If we have to handle a wild horse, it can never be wild again."

"Why not?" Preston asked. "That seems mean."

"I know it can. But it's not good for the rest of the herd if we do that. Horses are social animals. It's not easy, but they adjust. Just like people."

Preston listened with fascination to everything that Dash said. The boy seemed thrilled when he was allowed to first brush one of the mares and then sit on top of her.

Seeing the horses through the eyes of a child brought an unexpected satisfaction. The horses were what had drawn Dash to this place three years ago. None of his friends back home could believe that he was working here now. It was a total one-eighty from his old life.

Preston paused and glanced up at Shadrach, who poked his nose over the door before sneezing. "Why'd you name him Shadrach?"

"This guy and two other horses were in some stables in Virginia when a fire broke out. Miraculously, they made it out untouched. They were promptly named Shadrach, Meshach, and Abednego. Do you know who they are?"

"From the Bible?"

"That's right. They trusted God in the fiery furnace and came out unscathed."

Preston grinned and patted the mare's neck. "I like that. I want to work here when I grow up."

Dash put his hands on his hips. "Maybe you can then. It's a great job."

"*And* you get to search for the bad guys?"

"I do."

"That sounds dangerous." The boy's voice held an air of wonder.

Dash glanced at Lizzie and saw the frown flicker across her face. Probably no mother liked to think of their child as being in the line of danger. Dash couldn't blame her.

But, mostly, his job was uneventful. The island

had very little crime. But that didn't mean Dash didn't have to be ready to face down the bad guys at any moment.

"We should probably get going." Lizzie pointed toward the door.

A twinge of regret filled Dash as their time came to an end. Today had been a nice change of pace. "Of course."

"Thanks again for everything." Lizzie looked up at him, her brown eyes full of warmth and gratitude. "I really appreciate it. Preston had a wonderful time."

Part of Dash wanted to think of another excuse to spend more time with this woman while she was here. But he didn't want to cross any professional lines. It was best if he kept his distance—for more than one reason.

He wasn't looking for romance. The last woman he'd dated had crushed his heart. Dash should have seen the signs. His friends had even tried to warn him. But Dash had only seen what he wanted to see. Wasn't that the way it worked with love so often?

Still, Dash didn't want to make those mistakes again.

Finally, he gave the mother and son a nod. "Enjoy the rest of your time on the island."

He shut the door on any future possibility of seeing them. That was the only smart thing that he could do.

But instead of feeling proud of himself, Dash felt a rush of disappointment.

THEIR TIME with the horses had been surprisingly fun. Lizzie hadn't expected to enjoy herself, but she had. Seeing Preston so engaged had brought immeasurable comfort to her heart.

She only wanted the best for her child.

It was the main reason she'd come here to Cape Corral.

But now she needed to head back to her cottage and figure out what to fill the rest of her day with.

"Come on, Preston." Lizzie motioned to her truck.

She'd actually only owned the truck for a day. It was a long story, but getting to the island had been quite the ordeal. The bridge leading to Cape Corral had washed out in a storm a couple of months ago. So, now, to get here people had to take a boat from the mainland.

Since Lizzie had come at the last minute, plan-

BREAKWATER PROTECTOR   61

ning had been nearly nonexistent. She had arranged to sell her car and met the buyer at the harbor. After pocketing the money, she waited for a boat to take her and Preston over to Cape Corral.

While on the boat, she'd talked to the captain, who told her about someone selling one of his four-wheel-drive vehicles on the island. It had taken some arranging, but Lizzie had managed to make it to the man's house, purchased the truck with cash, and drove herself back to the cottage she'd rented.

The truck hadn't been exactly everything she'd envisioned. It was rusty, had ripped seats, and a strange, musty odor filled the inside. But it would work for the time being.

The island didn't have any paved roads—only stretches of sand. There was no way to get around the area except with four-wheel drive, which Lizzie had only used in the snow.

She pulled on her seatbelt and cranked the engine, giving one last wave to Dash as he stood in the door of the Community Safety building.

She put the vehicle in Drive and started forward.

But her tires spun in the soft sand.

"No, no, no!" She didn't want this to happen now, not in front of Dash. She'd already asked too much of him. Now it looked like she'd need his help again.

Lizzie was used to being the self-sufficient one. The one who helped other people. But now she was the one who needed help—over and over again. Was God trying to give her a big dose of humility?

She pressed the accelerator harder.

Her tires continued to spin in place.

What should she do? Lizzie hadn't exactly read up on this before she left her home. Should she back up and try to speed forward? Was she pressing the accelerator too hard?

"Mom?" Preston asked.

"Just give me a minute."

She had no idea the correct way to fix this, and her cheeks heated when she realized that she had an audience. Dash and another man stood outside the Community Building watching her fiasco.

Earlier, when no one had been around, she'd had no problems driving.

If there was one thing these past two months had taught her, it was that she wasn't as tough as she'd thought. She'd realized her weaknesses . . . and most of her realizations were caused by fear.

CHAPTER EIGHT

"HEY! HOLD UP." Dash waved Lizzie down before she burned up her engine.

The woman obviously had no idea how to drive in this terrain. Then again, most people didn't.

Some beaches in other parts of the country had hard, packed sand that even a sedan could drive on. But the sand in Cape Corral was so soft that it was like granules of sugar. Drivers not only had to have a four-wheel-drive vehicle but also had to air down their tires to at least 20 PSI. Dash was surprised at the number of people who came here not knowing that before they tried to drive through this sandy town.

"Looks like you need a hand." Dash strode toward Lizzie's truck.

Her very beat-up truck. In fact, this looked a lot like Mr. Henderson's old F150.

"Should I just accelerate more?" Lizzie's expression was nearly stoic as she stared at him.

"No, you don't want to do that. You're just going to bury yourself deeper. We're going to need to dig you out. Did you air down your tires?"

She shrugged. "This is how they were when I got the truck. The previous owner showed me how to put it into four-wheel drive before I paid him. But that's it."

"Mr. Henderson?"

"I think that was his name."

Dash's questions about this woman continued to grow. How in the world was she connected with Mr. Henderson?

The man had lived on the island practically since the town had been settled. Not really, but he *was* as local as they came. He had the weathered skin and salty manners to prove it.

The man was also a miser who liked to make money however he could—including by selling things he found in other people's trash for top dollars. He'd tried to peddle video cameras that couldn't record, rafts with holes in them, and once he'd been caught trying to sell three-day-old muffins that had been tossed from the local market.

Lizzie seemed like a smart lady, like the type who'd know better than to be in a situation like this. Then again, Dash really didn't know that much about her.

"Why don't you hop out?" he said. "Let me see what I can do."

Thirty minutes later, Dash had gotten the truck out of the sand and given Lizzie a few lessons on how to drive on the island.

But the woman still looked nervous, and Dash wasn't sure if she was comfortable driving back to her place alone.

Dash spotted Levi stepping from the Community Safety building and yelled to him. "Hey, man! Could you pick me up in about fifteen minutes over at the old Dawson place?"

His friend paused and nodded. "Sure thing. Everything okay?"

"I'm just going to ride with Ms. McCreary to make sure she gets home okay."

"Got it," Levi said.

Dash climbed in the truck and indicated that Lizzie should keep driving.

The look she gave him clearly showed she'd lost confidence in her skills.

"There's nothing to be nervous about," Dash assured her. "Just take it slow and steady."

She released a long breath before pressing the accelerator again.

"That's right," Dash told her. "You can do this. Keep pressing the accelerator but not too hard."

Lizzie did just as he said.

They rolled through the sand, tires bouncing over the ruts and ridges. They made it over the first hill—the one that Lizzie had mentioned made her nervous—and continued toward her rental.

"There you go." Dash leaned back, ready to enjoy the rest of the ride. "You did it."

"Don't pat me on the back too soon," Lizzie murmured. "I've got a ways farther until I get back to my place. It's a wonder I was able to get to the station this morning."

"Sometimes it just depends on where you go in the sand. Or maybe you were just lucky this morning."

"Lucky is not something that most people call me." She looked as if she fought a frown.

Dash was tempted to ask her what that meant, but he didn't. It was better if he didn't ask too many personal questions. Distance would be his friend.

He directed Lizzie to cut over to a road leading to the ocean. The sand—and open area—here were easier to navigate for inexperienced drivers.

Preston squealed beside him, obviously enjoying the ride. Dash himself remembered going off-roading on the beach as a child. It had been one of his favorite things also. There was nothing like feeling the ocean breeze float through your windows and listening to the waves crash as you cruised over the sand.

"Why are there rocks in the water?" Preston pointed to a jetty in the distance.

"That's called a breakwater," Dash explained. "Some people call them jetties. They're erected to protect the island from erosion. We were losing too much shoreline for a while."

"It looks out of place."

Dash couldn't argue with that. "It does, but it still serves an important purpose."

A lot of pieces needed to be in place to properly guard this island—everything from the breakwater at the ocean's edge to the saltwater cowboys who made sure humans didn't impede on the horses and their habitat. Dash felt honored to be a part of it all.

As the wind floated through the windows, Dash caught a whiff of Lizzie's coconut shampoo. Was that the vague scent of vanilla also? The aroma combination was surprisingly pleasing.

But Dash would be better off if he hadn't noticed.

"I should have never bought this piece of junk," Lizzie muttered as the truck started to stall again. She managed to shift it into a lower gear and keep moving.

"The truth is, vehicles around here usually last only around four years."

"Why is that?" Lizzie quickly stole a glance at him. "It seems like a travesty."

"Between the saltwater and the wear and tear brought by driving on the sand, vehicles wear out quickly. The elements are harsh on them, to say the least."

"How old do you think this truck is?"

Dash shrugged. "This one? Oh, I'd guess it's thirty years old. At least."

Her bottom lip dropped. "How is it even still running?"

"That's a great question. My friends and I were wondering that too."

They reached Lizzie's house, and she put the truck in Park.

"I did it," she announced, the tautness gone from her voice.

Dash saw the victory in her eyes and couldn't help but smile. "You did. Good job."

Lizzie turned to him, not trying to hide her gratitude. "Thanks again. I feel like I keep saying that, but I really do owe you."

The sight of her made his breath catch. She really was a sight to behold. Her dark hair had just enough body to make styling it look effortless. Her olive skin was flawless. Her profile made a lovely silhouette.

He hadn't found himself this captivated by a woman in a long time.

"You don't owe me anything. I'm glad I could help."

As they wrapped up their conversation, Preston hopped out and started skipping toward the house.

"I'll be right there, Preston!" Lizzie called, scrambling after him. She paused before crossing the sand and glanced at Dash. "Would you like to come inside for some water while you wait for your friend to pick you up?"

He considered it briefly. "I guess that would beat waiting outside by myself. Why not?"

Dash reminded himself to keep his distance as he followed her inside.

This was just a friendly visit and nothing else.

But, if that was the truth, why did he have to keep telling himself that?

———————

LIZZIE SHOULDN'T HAVE INVITED Dash in. Yet she couldn't leave him outside alone after he'd helped her out.

Still, she reminded herself not to get too close. Doing so would be a mistake.

Dash lingered behind her as she climbed the steps to the cottage. Once she punched in her code, Dash grabbed the door so she could step inside.

But as soon as she did, she froze. The hairs on her arms rose.

Something was different inside.

Had someone been here while she was gone?

She glanced around, looking for a clue. Looking for a sign about what had made her senses go on alert.

Everything looked the same—the pastel-hued pictures still hung on the walls, and the white wicker furniture was in place. Still, something had set off that feeling. But what?

"You look like you've seen a ghost, Mom." Preston gazed up at her in curiosity.

The boy had always been able to read her much better than Lizzie ever thought he should.

"I'm fine." But her voice didn't sound convincing.

Dash stepped up behind her and glanced around also. "You sure everything's okay? You do look a little pale, just like the P-man said."

The P-man? Lizzie didn't even have time to ask about that now. Not when danger could be close. "I know I'm going to sound crazy, but something feels off."

"Would you like for me to take a look around?"

Everything inside her wanted to say yes. But the less this man knew about her, the better.

Lizzie attempted to pull herself together and act like this was no big deal as she waved her hand in the air. "I'm sure everything's fine."

"I'll take a look around anyway." Before she could object, Dash searched the kitchen.

He must not have seen anything because he had no reaction.

As he walked past her, he pointed to the stairs.

"I'm just going to peek up here real quick. Nothing too nosy."

Lizzie nodded, one part of her wanting to object, and the other part of her totally relieved.

A few minutes later, Dash came back downstairs and paused in front of her. "I'm not seeing anything out of the ordinary. The only thing I noticed was a card here on the kitchen table."

Everything went still around her at his words. "A card?"

"A business card from the management company that oversees the house," he explained. "I didn't pick it up and read it. Sometimes, their employees stop by because of a maintenance issue or something. They leave a card with a little note scribbled on the back. Why don't you take a look?"

She nodded at Dash—she *thought* she nodded, at least—as she walked over to the kitchen table and picked up the card. On the front was a smiling picture of an agent named Mary Lou Hoskins, who was with the management company.

As Lizzie flipped the card over, a handwritten note greeted her.

Tried to call. No one answered. Had to come by and check on a potential leak. Owner had high water bill. All is good. Thanks—Mary Lou.

Lizzie released the breath that she held.

Somebody *had* been inside. She wasn't going crazy.

But, thank goodness, it was just a routine maintenance call.

When would she stop feeling so paranoid?

Lizzie was afraid that the answer was never.

CHAPTER NINE

SOMETHING WAS DEFINITELY GOING on with Lizzie, Dash thought as he waved goodbye and climbed into the Jeep with Levi. People didn't go pale like that for no reason.

Had the woman come to Cape Corral to escape from something?

His gut indicated the answer was yes.

The thing he wasn't sure about was what.

Dash should leave the subject alone. Lizzie's life wasn't his business. But he couldn't stop thinking about it either.

"Everything okay?" Levi asked as they pulled away.

"I guess." He shrugged and glanced out the window. "That woman is skittish, though."

Levi glanced back at her house. "Any idea what's going on?"

"No, but she bought that truck from Mr. Henderson."

"I wouldn't buy chicken eggs from Mr. Henderson. How in the world did she end up buying his truck?" Levi shoved his eyebrows together.

"That's what I would like to know. Maybe I'll ask when I have the chance."

"Where did she come here from?" Levi asked.

"She said Maryland. But she was vague. Not to mention the fact that she quickly jumped in to answer before her son could."

"Interesting. We should probably keep an eye on the situation. We don't want any more trouble coming to Cape Corral."

"Not after that last fiasco, we don't." Dash frowned.

They'd found a dead man buried in the sand and a woman with amnesia who washed ashore.

The good news was that Levi and the woman had ended up becoming close, and she was living here in Cape Corral now. All in all, it hadn't been a complete disaster.

"Maybe you could do a little digging and find out what's going on," Levi suggested.

Dash raised his eyebrows. "What do you mean?"

"I mean, if you run into Lizzie again, see if she'll share anything else with you. Maybe you can put the pieces together."

Interesting proposition. "I'm not sure that woman is going to say anything to me. She clams up tighter than a shellfish during low tide."

"I'm just saying, it can't hurt to fish for information. Not because you're nosy but because, if danger is following her, we need to know about it."

"Point taken."

Levi hit the brakes as they approached a crowd. Several held signs, it appeared, as they paced on an empty lot of land.

"What's going on up there?" Dash muttered.

Levi hunched as he tried to get a better look. "Some locals are protesting the land that's being bought up."

"Protesting?" Surprise raced through Dash. "That's the first I've heard of it."

"People are getting fed up with the prospect of more development here. They suspect the county doesn't have our town's best interests at heart. They decided to practice their right to peacefully protest."

"Do you know who's buying the land?"

Levi shrugged. "Do I know for sure? No. But I suspect it's the Fergusons."

Dash nodded slowly. That's what he'd expected Levi to say.

For now, he would let his friend think that. But he knew the truth was on the verge of exploding.

"MOM, LOOK! LOOK!"

Based on the urgency in Preston's voice, more tension threaded up Lizzie's spine.

Was trouble here yet again?

She rushed from the kitchen table where she'd set up her workstation and dashed out the front door. Preston had left it open when he stepped onto the deck, and Lizzie hadn't complained. At least she could see and hear him that way.

He pointed to something beneath the house. "Horses. Wild horses!"

Lizzie sucked in a breath as she glanced down. Sure enough, two mares stood beneath the house, grazing on some sea oats. The creatures were beautiful. Stunning.

She tried to remember everything she'd read

about them in a booklet that had been left in the cottage.

Apparently, the horses had been here for hundreds of years. They'd come over from Europe and the vessels carrying them had overturned. But the horses had made it to shore, and they'd been here ever since. Spanish mustangs, if she remembered correctly.

There were instructions all over the island reminding people not to touch them, try to ride them, or feed them. In fact, people could be fined if they got any closer than fifty feet to the creatures.

"Can I go down and touch one?" Preston asked.

"No, sweetie. That's against the rules."

"But why?"

"Maybe that's a question you can ask Dash some-time." Now why had she said that? The chances were, they might not see the man again. She swallowed hard, trying to correct herself. "I think, most of the time, officials don't want people handling wild animals for various reasons. I'm sure these horses can be dangerous."

"They look peaceful."

"But wild animals are still wild animals," Lizzie reminded him. "They're unpredictable. The last thing you want is for one of them to kick you."

Preston frowned and continued leaning over the deck rail to look at the horses.

Lizzie bent over the railing also, soaking in the magnificent creatures.

As she did, she saw a set of footprints in the sand beneath her house.

Her spine tightened.

Where did those come from? They were to the side of the house, away from where Dash had walked when he'd brought her back here. They were too big to belong to Preston and too wide to belong to her.

Lizzie was nearly certain they hadn't been there earlier. She'd walked around the entire place when she'd first arrived, checking things out to make sure it was safe.

A bad feeling brewed in her gut. What if someone had been outside? What if someone had been checking out this place?

Maybe Lizzie needed to take a picture of those prints. They could be evidence in case anything happened . . . though she prayed that wouldn't be the case.

Just as Lizzie pulled out her phone to take a snapshot, one of the horses walked right over the area.

No!

The footprints were gone.

But Lizzie wouldn't forget that they had been there. It would be unwise to do so.

Especially in light of everything that had happened.

CHAPTER TEN

WHY HAD that man come to Lizzie's place again?

The law officer was getting too close to her.

The thought made his blood boil.

If Lizzie and Preston were all alone, his plan would work perfectly.

But if someone else got involved . . . things would be complicated.

He'd already gone inside her place while she was gone. He'd looked around. Made notes about exits and potential self-defense weapons. He'd checked her computer. Smelled her clothes. Laid his head on her pillow.

A smile curled his lips at the thought.

And she had no idea.

Part of him wanted to simply storm into the house and claim what was his.

But he couldn't do that.

No, he needed to be patient. Soon enough, his plan would come to fruition.

He just had to wait.

In the shadows.

Watching.

Until it was time to pounce.

CHAPTER ELEVEN

"MOM, I'm tired of staying inside. We haven't left the house in three days."

Lizzie glanced at Preston and frowned. She knew exactly where he was coming from.

The two of them hadn't gone anywhere since they'd visited the stable with Dash.

That also meant they'd had three peaceful days at home without any incidents.

The two of them had fallen into a nice routine. Preston had done his schoolwork. Lizzie had worked in between his assignments. They cooked everything at home instead of going out to eat. They'd even taken little walks up and down the street and marveled at the occasional wild horse.

The change was nice.

But Lizzie knew exactly what Preston was talking about when he said he was getting cabin fever. The problem was, where would they go? There were no movie theaters here. It was too cold to go into the ocean. No arcades or mini-golf courses were close— nothing that they might entertain themselves with like back home.

"What would you like to do, honey?" She leaned toward him as they sat at the kitchen table and waited for his response.

His gaze brightened. "It's Sunday. How about church?"

Lizzie's eyebrows shot up. She should have been the one who thought about that. They'd been regular attenders back at home. But when they'd come to the island, she'd just assumed they would stay to themselves and maybe watch a church service online. The fewer people they were around, the better.

But Lizzie also knew they couldn't live like this forever. Eventually, she and Preston were going to have to rejoin the land of the living.

It *would* be nice to see other people. Though she was okay being alone, another part of her craved human interaction.

Maybe part of her had even hoped that Dash might stop by again.

But he hadn't.

Lizzie shouldn't be disappointed over that, but there was a sliver of the emotion inside her. The man had been nice and attentive, and Preston liked him. Plus, it was good to have one person in town who knew she was here, just in case anything happened.

She shuddered at the thought.

In case anything happened . . . she prayed it didn't come to that.

"I guess I need to look up what churches are here and what time they start." She pushed her reading glasses up higher on her nose as she looked at Preston. "You think I can drive there?"

"Mr. Dash taught you how to. Of course you can." Preston nodded confidently.

Lizzie smiled when she heard the total faith in her son's voice. She hoped she didn't let the boy down. For that matter, she hoped coming to Cape Corral wasn't a terrible idea.

Everything she'd done was for Preston. But the path to safety wasn't always a clear one. She hoped and prayed that she didn't regret her hideout. But there hadn't been a better choice.

"I'll look up a church around here, sweetie."

She opened her computer and did a quick search. Based on everything she saw, there was only one here on the island, Cape Corral Community. She glanced at the map and thought she could navigate her way there. But the service started in forty-five minutes, and, if they were going to make it in time, they needed to leave soon.

Another shudder of nerves rushed through her.

She hoped she was making a wise choice by going out in public.

Because she hated regrets, and she already had a long list.

DASH DID a double take when he looked over while singing the closing hymn and saw Lizzie and Preston standing in the back of the little sanctuary. Just as he saw her, she looked over, seeming to feel his eyes on her. Dash tilted his head in silent greeting.

As a reward, he got a smile from her.

The sight of it shouldn't make Dash feel delighted. But it did.

As soon as the pastor said amen and dismissed everybody, Dash strode toward the twosome. He tousled Preston's hair, immediately getting a prompt smile from the boy. "How are you doing, P-man?"

"Doing good. Lots of schoolwork. It's exhausting."

Dash fought a smile. The boy almost sounded like an old man who worked too much.

"It sounds like you're doing some good stuff then." Dash glanced up at Lizzie. "And how are you?"

"I can't complain."

She looked lovely today. Then again, Lizzie looked lovely every time Dash had seen her. But the black skirt and olive-green top really brought out her skin tones. She'd even worn earrings and a necklace to match.

"I didn't see you come in," Dash continued.

"We got here a little late," Lizzie said. "Even though you're a great driving instructor, it still took me a little while to manage these roads. But I made it."

"She got stuck once," Preston offered.

"Preston! Don't share all my secrets," she said with a scolding smile.

"But we did," the boy insisted.

"Did she figure out how to get out of it?" Dash glanced from Preston to Lizzie.

"I did what you told me, and I somehow managed to keep going through the sand. Thank goodness—especially since my cell service is spotty out here at best."

"Yes, thank goodness indeed."

People jostled around them as they left the small church building. Several older ladies stopped to give Dash a hug. As they did, the scent of their pungent perfumes filled his nostrils. Thankfully, Lizzie and Preston still lingered. He didn't want to miss the opportunity to catch up.

Or the opportunity to find out why they were here.

Levi was right—it was important to monitor everything going on here in Cape Corral.

"Hey, Dash!" a female voice said.

He turned to see Emmy Sutherland standing there. She was Levi's sister and a good friend. She had a way about her that made everyone feel like her best friend. "Hey, Emmy. What's going on?"

Her wholesome face lit up with a welcoming grin. "I cooked some fried chicken for everybody for lunch. I'm hoping you'll come over and join us."

"You know I can't pass up fried chicken." Fried chicken was Dash's weakness.

"So you'll be there?"

"Wouldn't miss it."

"Great." Emmy's gaze went to Lizzie and Preston, and she offered another smile. "Bring your friends."

"Oh, these are . . ." Dash tried to figure out how to describe who they were in relationship to him without sounding awkward. Before he could find the words, Lizzie extended her hand.

"I'm Lizzie, and this is my son, Preston. We're just here visiting for a while."

"I'm Emmy." The woman paused. "I'm surprised I haven't seen you around."

Lizzie shrugged, that guarded look returning to her gaze. "What can I say? I wish we were on vacation. But Preston and I have had lots of schoolwork to keep us busy."

"I can imagine. We would love to have you over for lunch, but I understand if you can't make it. If not today, we can do it another time."

Lizzie nodded, her shoulders relaxing ever so slightly. "Let me talk to my son. Thank you for the invitation."

Emmy waved. "No problem. I hope to see you today, but otherwise I'll catch you guys around."

Dash glanced back up at Lizzie as Emmy hurried out the door and down the steps. "What do you think?"

"I don't know . . ." She looped a tendril of hair behind her ear.

"We should do it, Mom." Preston tugged on her arm. "You know how much I love talking to people."

Dash leaned closer. "And Emmy has a whole colony of feral cats in her backyard."

Preston's eyes widened. "What's a feral cat? Are they scary? Do I have to get fifty shots if one bites me?"

Dash chuckled. "No, they're not scary. They're just stray cats who've made colonies for themselves in the woods. They're pretty fascinating to watch. I doubt any of them have rabies."

"It's sad that they don't have a home." Preston frowned.

"They love it. Just like our horses around here love it. Besides, Emmy can't resist herself. She feeds them and gives them water. And our island vet checks them out whenever needed to make sure they're healthy and not hurt."

"Well, that's good, at least." Preston turned back to his mother, an even more determined look in his eyes now. "So can we?"

Lizzie hesitated another moment before nodding. "Why not?"

CHAPTER TWELVE

LIZZIE TOOK her time as she walked toward Dash's truck. She had planned on driving to lunch, but Dash insisted on giving them a ride and bringing them back to their truck when the meal was over.

Lizzie wasn't going to argue. She definitely didn't want to drive that truck any more than she had to. She'd been hesitant since being stuck.

It had been nice of Emmy to extend the invitation to her and Preston. Perhaps Lizzie had lived in the city for so long that she forgot what small-town hospitality was like. It was refreshing, actually.

Even though Lizzie wanted to stay to herself and not make herself known around town, she knew that the longer she remained here, the more that would be an impossibility. Her only hope was that, since she was here on this island cut off from the rest of the world, that maybe the rest of the world was cut off from the island as well. She'd taken all the precautions so nobody would find her here.

Not *anyone*. But especially a certain someone.

"Emmy seems nice," Lizzie commented as she, Dash, and Preston strolled through the sand toward his truck.

"She's great," Dash said. "Her brother heads the Forestry Division here on the island. Name's Levi. You saw him at the station the other day."

"Yes, I remember him. He picked you up."

"That's right. Levi's father held Levi's position before Levi took over a few years ago. Their family goes way back here on the island."

"But you said you don't, correct?" Lizzie had to admit she was curious about this man. "You're a more recent transplant?"

Dash rubbed the back of his neck. "That's right. I actually had an office job, and I hated it. I decided I needed a change, and I remembered coming here to Cape Corral as a child. I decided to take the plunge and start over."

She admired his courage in doing that. Would she be brave enough to stay here for good? It was only supposed to be a stop along the way.

"Was it a good choice?" she finally asked.

"It was a great choice. I haven't regretted it once."

Lizzie smiled, a moment of envy shooting through her. She hoped, if it ever came down to it, she would feel the same confidence.

As they reached Dash's truck, his eyes darkened. Lizzie followed his gaze and saw a paper tucked under his windshield. Without saying anything, Dash quickly plucked it from beneath the windshield wiper and glanced at the words scrawled there.

His entire body tensed, and he glanced around.

What could have caused his reaction? Lizzie wondered.

Maybe going somewhere with him wasn't a great idea. Not if he was harboring secrets that made him look so on edge.

DASH COULDN'T GET the note out of his mind as he ate with Emmy and the gang.

The message left on his windshield had been simple.

I know what you're doing.

But who had left the paper there? Who had found out about his plan?

Dash had no idea, and he found it hard to keep his focus on the conversation at the dinner table around him.

Any other time, this meal would have been fun. The gang from Fire and Rescue, as well as from the Forestry Division, all hung out at Emmy's place. She owned the inn in town.

She was a great cook, and her fried chicken rivaled Mrs. Minnie's—not that anybody would ever dare to say that to Mrs. Minnie. The town's restaurateur took her position very seriously.

Lizzie and Preston seemed to fit right in. Preston dove into conversations and entertained everyone with his random thoughts. Lizzie, on the other hand, was more standoffish. She didn't look uncomfortable, more like she was soaking everything in.

Dash still wondered exactly what was going on with her. There was obviously more to her story than she let on.

What he should really do was forget about this woman and her son. That had been his goal all along. Not to get too close. But these two kept showing up in his life. And part of him wanted to reach out to them with open arms.

"Any updates on who's buying the properties up on the island?" Grant asked, picking up another homemade biscuit and slathering some butter on it.

Dash tensed at the question.

"What I guess is that the Fergusons set up some type of shell organization and they're the ones buying it." Colby shrugged.

Colby was a firefighter and Emmy's best friend. The man was mischievous and boyish but dependable.

"That family is determined to turn this place into a resort." Levi frowned and shook his head. "We don't have the infrastructure for it, and it wouldn't be good for the horses."

"Who are the Fergusons?" Lizzie wiped her mouth with a napkin as she waited for a response.

"There's a bit of a feud going on here on the island," Dash explained. "The Fergusons moved here about a decade ago, and they're loaded, to say the least. They see a lot of potential investment property here on this island, and they've been fighting hard to build a resort up on the North End, near where they live."

"That would mean more tax revenue, right?" Lizzie asked. "But I take it that's not what you want."

"The new resort would mean a lot more traffic,

and the growth would mean less space for the wild horses," Grant explained. "They weren't meant to live on a busy island. Once, before the storm destroyed the bridge leading to Cape Corral, a few of the horses wandered down south. They actually walked right through the automatic doors in a grocery store before we were able to round up the horses."

Lizzie gasped. "Are you serious?"

"Serious as a heart attack. Thankfully, we were able to wrangle the horses and get them back here."

Lizzie frowned, her intelligent eyes flickering as she seemed to process the information. "So you think the Fergusons are secretly buying land so they can somehow get around the ordinances that are in place?"

She had a better understanding of this than Dash thought she would. The situation here was complicated. The Ferguson family was backstabbing, manipulative, and tried to use their money to buy whatever they wanted.

"That's how it appears." Dash chose his words carefully.

"I'm sorry to hear that." Lizzie frowned as if she truly meant the words. "This area is beautiful. I would hate to see it change too much. Some things are just meant to stay the way they are, you know?"

"You're going to fit right in with this group." Levi pointed at her with a fork laden with green beans. "Because that's the way we all think."

Dash grimaced.

How long would he be able to keep his secret a secret?

He wasn't sure.

Because he hated the guilt it brought with it.

CHAPTER THIRTEEN

LIZZIE COULDN'T BELIEVE how much she enjoyed her lunch at Emmy's. She hadn't expected to have fun. But being around people was nice. These *people* were nice.

For a minute, she tried to picture herself fitting in here. Not just for this brief amount of time she'd planned on being here. But for longer.

Could she see herself working here? Almost all her job responsibilities were online, so it was a possibility. Preston certainly seemed to enjoy being outdoors. Coming here seemed like a good decision in that sense.

Preston especially seemed to like Dash.

Her gaze wandered across the room to where Preston and Dash were talking about something.

Dash made a motion, almost like he was demonstrating how to fish with an invisible rod.

Seeing the two of them together made her smile. But she didn't want Preston to be crushed when they left here one day. Because, inevitably, that was going to happen.

"Your son is great," somebody said beside her.

She looked up to see a woman with long, dark wavy hair standing there. "Dani, right?"

"That's me. I'm one of the newer transplants to this island. This place still amazes me also."

She'd seen Dani talking to Levi earlier. From the way the two looked at each other, they appeared to be a couple.

"It certainly seems like a great group of people that you have here," Lizzie finally said.

"Oh, they are. They've all been so welcoming. Honestly, I don't remember when I was last this happy."

Dani's words made Lizzie smile—and envy her. "It's good to find a place that makes you happy."

"And people who make you happy," she quipped before shrugging. "Anyway, if you need anything while you're here, let me know."

"I'll do that."

But Lizzie might not be staying long enough for

that. Although the place fascinated her, she had bigger worries.

And she would go wherever she needed to go in order to get away from Nicolai.

———

"I'M GOING to go ask my mom!" Preston announced before bounding across the room.

Dash fought a smile as he watched the boy rush toward his mother like a heat-seeking missile finding its target. That boy was that kind of force.

What Dash wouldn't do to have that kind of enthusiasm.

A moment later, Preston took his mom by the hand and led her through the crowd back to Dash.

"Dash said it was okay," Preston said. "Right, Dash?"

"I said it was up to your mom," Dash clarified. "But I'd be more than happy to take Preston fishing. He says he's never been."

Lizzie tilted her head as she looked down at her son. "I hope you didn't invite yourself to do this or volunteer Dash."

"He didn't," Dash insisted. "Fishing is one of my favorite things to do, and today just happens to be my day off. I'd be happy to take him. You can come too if you'd like."

She didn't say anything for a moment. Instead, she stood there as if contemplating her options.

Dash fully expected her to make up an excuse and say no.

Instead, she shrugged and slowly nodded. "You know what? That sounds fun. Why not?"

Surprise—and delight—spread through him. "Great. Do you guys need to go back and change?"

Lizzie looked down at what appeared to be her designer outfit. "Probably a good idea. I'll look like a fish out of water in this outfit."

Preston rolled his eyes. "Not a mom pun . . . they're the worst!"

Dash fought a smile.

"I'll take you to your truck at the church and then follow you back to your house," Dash said. "You can ride with me to my favorite fishing hole. There's no need for both of us to drive."

"That sounds great. Just let me know if I need to bring anything. Otherwise, let's . . . open this can of worms." She winced as she looked at Preston. "Sorry —it just slipped out."

Preston groaned.

"Apology accepted." Dash winked at Lizzie. "Just

don't let it happen again—next time, we won't let you off the hook."

"SO, you hold the rod like this, flick your wrist back, and then you release the line into the water," Dash said as he instructed Preston on how to position his fishing pole.

Lizzie watched as Dash stood by Preston, one arm around him, and helped him cast his line into the water.

The area where Dash had brought them was secluded—and, if she'd calculated correctly, was on the edge of the notorious Wash Woods. This section of the forest was farther away from the section near her rental. A small channel came in from the Currituck Sound, and Dash had told them the brackish water was surprisingly deep here.

Maritime forest surrounded them, though the land was clear near the water. Still, prickly grass shot up and tickled their ankles. Small crabs darted in and out of the water near its edge. A heron minded its own business near some marsh grass.

Peaceful yet frightening. Such an odd combination. But that was also how Lizzie felt. Fascinated by this area yet terrified that something would go wrong.

"Now what?" Preston looked back as he stood holding the rod.

"Now you wait," Dash said. "So much of fishing is just waiting and thinking."

Preston frowned. "I don't like thinking."

"But it's a good skill to learn," Dash said. "Sometimes you have to embrace the quiet in order to figure out things in your life."

Preston grunted and turned back to the water with a shrug.

Her son would be happy for a few minutes, at least. But Lizzie was interested to see how her little boy, who often bounced off the walls, did while fishing.

"So this is your fishing hole, huh?" Lizzie asked as Dash stepped back to stand with her.

He rubbed his jaw as he stared out at the water, his cowboy hat shading his eyes. "I've done some of my best fishing here. Bluefish *love* these waters. Besides, it reminds me a little of home."

"Where is home?"

"West Virginia."

She raised her eyebrows. "Really? I didn't hear an accent."

He shrugged. "What can I say? I didn't grow up in the hollows—hollers, as some people call them—there. I wasn't terribly far from the DC area, actually."

"Sounds nice."

"It was. I loved fishing whenever I had the chance. In the lakes, in the streams, wherever I could. Fishing helped me to figure out life."

Lizzie glanced back at Preston as he hummed to himself while he fished. "What do you do with whatever you catch? Do you throw them back?"

Dash chuckled. "Throw them back? No. I cook them. Of course."

She rumpled her lips and nose. "So that means you have to clean and scale them, right?"

Dash let out a chuckle. "That's right. It all kind of goes hand in hand. You're telling me you've never done this?"

Lizzie shrugged. "I guess you could say I'm more of a city girl. I grew up in the suburbs around Philadelphia."

"Your parents still there?"

"No, they actually moved down to Florida. They didn't like the cold winters in Pennsylvania anymore." She would have escaped down to their place, but she didn't want to put them in danger.

"Can't blame them for not liking snow."

"I've never been much of a cold weather person either."

Dash shifted, his gaze narrowed with both amusement and challenge as he glanced at Preston. "Tell you what. If Preston catches a fish, I'll teach you how to clean it and cook it."

"I'm not sure if that makes me want him to catch a fish or not."

He chuckled again. "There's nothing that tastes quite as good as fresh fish."

Lizzie's gaze went to her son, and she smiled as he hummed to himself. "It's just nice to see him having fun."

Dash's eyes lingered on her a moment, almost as if he wanted to ask follow-up questions about her statement. But he didn't.

As she glanced back at Dash, she couldn't help but notice that he seemed somewhat familiar.

But why would someone like Dash be familiar to her? The thought was ridiculous. She'd never been to Cape Corral before. She had no reason to have ever crossed paths with him.

Dash must simply look like somebody she'd seen before. It was the only thing that made sense.

She cleared her throat, deciding to change the subject. "Your friends all seem nice."

"They're great," he said. "It's amazing how, when you can find something in common with other people, that cause can really bond you."

"What is the thing you all have in common? The wild horses?"

Dash shrugged. "Preserving this place. We all love this island."

"It's a good place to love." As she said the words, her gaze caught with Dash's, and something passed between them.

Lizzie tried to look away, but it was like she couldn't. She just wanted to study Dash, to learn everything she could about the man.

"I think I caught something!" Preston yelled, tugging on the fishing rod.

The moment was broken—and it was just as well. Lizzie wasn't even sure what the unspoken things between her and Dash were. It was better if she didn't find out.

Dash rushed over to help Preston reel his line in.

Lizzie held her breath. Would it be a fish? Would she find herself scaling one of those creatures before too long?

She still wasn't sure how she felt about doing that.

But as Preston waited to see what he'd hooked, the hair on Lizzie's neck rose.

She glanced at the woods surrounding them.

She saw nothing.

What was with this feeling? Why did she sense somebody watching her?

Lizzie glanced around again, trying to find the source of her feeling.

Still nothing.

She needed to be on guard.

Because letting her guard down could have a disastrous ending.

She'd be wise to never forget that.

CHAPTER FOURTEEN

"YOU GOT ONE!" Dash announced. "Great job, P-man."

Preston grinned as he stared at the fish wiggling at the end of his line.

"This is what we call a grey trout." Dash pulled the fish closer for a better look.

"I can't believe I caught something. I actually caught something! My friends back home won't believe this!"

Lizzie joined Dash and Preston on the banks. "That's great, sweetie. And it looks like a big one too."

"This is going to taste great for dinner one night." Dash pulled long-nosed pliers from his tacklebox.

"Now we've got to work on getting the hook from his mouth. You've got to be careful doing this because you don't want the hook to pierce your skin."

"Can I do it?" Preston looked up with those curious eyes of his.

Dash leveled his gaze with the boy. "Can you be careful?"

"Of course. I'm very careful." The boy's voice held absolute confidence.

Dash glanced at Lizzie and saw her frown as if uncertain about that answer.

But Dash would give the kid a chance. He handed him the pliers and showed him how to properly remove the hook from the fish's mouth.

A few moments later, the fish flopped at the bottom of a cooler.

"Now, I just need you to catch two more of those," Dash told Preston.

"Two more?" the boy asked.

"Well, you need enough for all of us to eat," Dash explained, enjoying watching the various expressions cross the boy's face—surprise, determination, curiosity.

"I guess that makes sense." He shrugged. "I'll do my best."

Dash grinned and stepped back, watching as Preston launched his fishing line into the water again. Good. Preston had listened to Dash's instructions and done exactly as he'd been taught.

As Dash glanced at Lizzie, he froze. Why was worry stretched across her pinched expression?

His grin disappeared. What had brought on the sudden change?

"Everything okay?" he asked.

She crossed her arms over her chest and stared at the woods in the distance. "I'm fine. Just not a nature girl, I suppose. I thought I heard something in the woods, and my mind went to worst-case scenarios."

She was probably thinking about that wild boar again. Dash couldn't blame her. After what she had experienced that first night he'd met her, anybody would be affected. But he couldn't help but wonder if there was more to what she said.

"I'll help keep my eyes open for trouble too."

She offered a slight but grateful smile. "Thank you. It seems that once you become a mom, the worrying doesn't stop."

"Cape Corral is pretty safe. But every place has its dangers."

"I suppose they do." She frowned again.

Before they could talk about it anymore, Preston yelled for them again.

He'd caught another fish.

———

LIZZIE FELT TORN between enjoying Preston's moment of triumph and wanting to run for dear life.

But she couldn't live always running away every time she heard a creak or had a bad feeling.

Instead, she continued studying the woods around her, looking for a sign that someone was out there.

There was no way Nicolai could have found them here, right? Lizzie had been so careful. She'd even changed her cell phone so, if there'd been any chance he could track her through the device, it would now be impossible since he didn't have her number.

When she looked at the facts, Lizzie knew she should be safe.

So why did her instincts tell her otherwise?

Another creak sounded in the woods, and Lizzie tensed.

Tension rippled through her muscles as her gaze probed the shadows between the trees.

She couldn't see anything. The foliage was too thick. The crevices between trees too dark. The entire area too wild and uninviting.

Anybody or anything could be hiding out there, the woods acting as an accomplice to their voyeurism.

Lizzie's throat tightened at the thought of it, at the realization of how exposed they were out here.

"I'm going to launch the line by myself again," Preston announced.

She glanced back in time to see Dash trying to guide her son.

But Preston wanted to do things his own way. That boy could jump in and think he knew exactly how to do everything.

As Preston jerked his rod back, a sharp pain pierced Lizzie's right hand and she cried out.

The pain turned into a tug.

She glanced down and saw the hook had caught her index finger.

Blood formed around the edges, and her finger started to swell.

Preston gasped and dropped the rod. Before he could get to her, Dash appeared at her side.

"That's why it's important to wait for me to give you instructions before you cast a line into the water," Dash said as he took Lizzie's hand into his calloused one.

"Mom, I'm so sorry. Are you okay? I didn't mean to. I promise. I didn't."

"I'm fine." But Lizzie couldn't stop staring at the hook going through her skin. Her head felt woozy at the sight of it. Blood always made her feel this way.

"We need to get this out of you."

"Please do." She closed her eyes and tried not to grimace.

"I'm going to try to slide this out," Dash said.

She still pressed her eyes closed. "Do whatever you have to do."

As Preston appeared on the other side of her and wrapped his arms around her waist, Lizzie forced her eyes open.

"I'm so sorry, Mom." Tears glimmered in his eyes.

"It's okay, sweetie. I know you didn't mean to." He didn't. The boy was just impulsive—just like her sister had been. Amanda had always acted and then thought. Their mom always said Amanda was the reason she'd gone gray early.

Lizzie felt Dash tugging at the hook and waited for her finger to be released, for this to be over with.

But all she felt was tugging and pulling—no real movement.

"This hook got you pretty good," Dash muttered. "I'm going to cut the line and see if I can slide it out. Let me just grab some tools."

As Dash stepped away, Lizzie squeezed Preston closer, happy to have someone to hold onto.

Then her eyes flung open, and she glanced across the woods again.

The sound.

She heard it again.

Someone or something was out there.

Whoever or whatever it was made her forget her temporary pain.

Dash appeared again. He cut the line and tried to work the hook out.

This time she didn't close her eyes.

Instead, Lizzie stared across the water into the woods on the other side. At any minute, she expected danger to appear.

"I'm going to need to get special pliers I have at my place," Dash said. "Why don't we all get back into my truck, and I'll take us there?"

As another snap sounded in the woods, Dash tensed. He'd heard it too this time. His gaze darted toward the sound.

Lizzie wasn't sure if the confirmation made her feel comforted or more frightened. Part of her hoped she'd just been imagining things.

"You two get into my truck," Dash said. "I'll get our stuff and be right there."

CHAPTER FIFTEEN

DASH FEARED Lizzie might pass out as he tugged at the hook latched onto her finger. He'd never seen one embedded quite this deep before and knew it had to be uncomfortable.

Lizzie had even sent Preston out into his backyard to play with Goliath, Dash's St. Bernard, so the boy didn't have to see her distress. Meanwhile, the two of them sat at his kitchen table, a first aid kit spread in front of them.

"You doing okay?" Dash studied her face, worried about the pallor of her skin.

"I'm fine." Despite her words, Lizzie's voice sounded thin and uncertain.

"I promise, you're going to survive." He kept his

voice light and teasing. "I guess you can officially say you're *hooked* on fishing now."

"I should have never set this precedent earlier. Fishing puns are the worst." Lizzie let out a weak chuckle before shaking her head. She pressed her eyes shut, and when she opened them again, moisture lined the edges.

Concern pulsed through him. "Am I hurting you this badly?"

"No, it's not that." Lizzie shrugged and drew in a shaky breath. "I mean, this doesn't feel great. Don't get me wrong. I just feel . . . I don't know. I guess I feel like I'm falling apart."

Dash sensed her words went much deeper than this situation. "What do you mean?"

"Let's see. My son almost got gored to death by a boar. I got stuck in quicksand, something I didn't even know existed outside of *The Princess Bride*. My truck, which I bought from a stranger, got stuck in the sand. And now here I am with a fishhook in my finger. It's not really an exaggeration to say it feels like nothing is going right."

"Well, if you're falling apart, then you're making falling apart look as graceful as a tree losing leaves in the autumn breeze."

Her gaze swerved to meet his, her pupils widening. "You didn't tell me you were a poet."

He grinned. "I'm just telling the truth."

"You're just being nice."

"I *have* been impressed by how you handled everything since you've arrived here."

She released a long breath and looked away from her finger. "It's just . . . back at home, I had everything together. As the saying goes, all of my ducks were in a row. But now . . . now I wonder how I ever did any of it. Not only are my ducks not in a row . . . they're running away in panic from an old man with a broom."

A smile tugged at his lips at her description. "You'll figure it out again."

Lizzie's gaze fluttered up to meet his. "Why do you sound so sure?"

"Because I can see it in your eyes. I like to think of myself as being a pretty good judge of character."

"I appreciate your confidence in me."

Just as she said the words, Dash pulled the hook from her finger. She flinched before relief filled her expression.

Lizzie lifted her finger, as if to examine it herself. "You did it."

"Of course." Dash stood and turned on the water

from the faucet. He called Lizzie over and held her hand under the stream, letting the moisture flood over her finger. "Now we just need to make sure you get it nice and clean."

Having Lizzie this close felt good. Even after being outside all day, Dash could still smell her coconut and vanilla scent. Her skin was soft under his touch, and her gaze was always intelligent.

Why was Dash having these feelings for the woman? It wasn't like him. He'd been so guarded lately.

But something about Lizzie was different.

As the thought circled in his head, Dash frowned.

He'd sworn off dating, but he felt so tempted right now.

Too tempted.

If he was smart, Dash would take Lizzie home and continue on with his life.

But instead, he found himself saying, "I have some leftover twelve-layer cake from Mrs. Minnie's. Would you and Preston like some?"

LIZZIE SHOULD HAVE SAID no to the cake. She should have asked Dash to take her home.

But for some reason, she said yes and stayed.

Not only did she enjoy the vanilla cake with chocolate icing, but afterward they'd decided to play Monopoly. The game had lasted entirely longer than Lizzie had expected—yet shorter than she would have liked it.

When the game finished, she, Dash, and Preston had sat down with some popcorn to watch a TV show Preston had told them about. The next thing they knew, Preston was snoozing on the loveseat.

"He's a tired boy," Lizzie said. "I guess today wore him out."

"It's all that fun he had out there fishing."

Lizzie smiled. "It is good to see him just being a boy. To be able to run and play and be outside. Back in—" She'd almost said New York but stopped herself. "Back in Maryland, there really wasn't much green space where we lived."

Dash turned to her, a curious gleam in his gaze. "Can I ask you something?"

A tinge of nerves fluttered through her. Asking questions could be dangerous. But Dash had done so much for her, how could she refuse?

Finally, she shrugged. "Maybe. It depends on the question."

He chuckled. "Fair enough. I know it's not my business, but is Preston's dad in his life?"

Lizzie could handle that question. "No, he's not. Preston has never met him, for that matter."

Dash said nothing, only waited. As he did, Lizzie wondered how much she should share.

Part of her wanted to open up. Wanted to tell him more.

Yet Preston's dad was someone she hardly ever talked about. Still, it would feel good to get things out in the open, especially with this man who'd done so much for her.

Lizzie licked her lips before starting. "Preston is actually my sister's child. Amanda was seventeen when she got pregnant. She never mentioned who the father was, nor did he ever come forward. Unfortunately, Amanda died during a complication of childbirth."

"I'm sorry to hear that."

Lizzie nodded, trying to hold back her emotions. The memories still felt fresh, even after all these years.

"So, long story short, I adopted Preston," she said.

"How old were you?"

"Nineteen."

Dash's eyebrows shot up. "That must have been a hard decision."

"Actually, it was a no brainer. I knew without a doubt that I was going to raise Preston. I was going to make my sister proud."

A new emotion passed through his gaze. He almost looked like . . . he admired her. The thought brought Lizzie surprising delight.

"How did you do it?" Dash asked. "How did you manage to raise a great boy and become who you are today?"

Lizzie pulled her legs beneath her as she faced Dash on the couch. "It was a lot of hard work and sleepless nights. I did college classes online mostly. My parents also helped me out when they could. I'm not really sure how Preston and I got through some of those days except for the grace of God."

"The grace of God can get us far, can't it?"

She smiled, grateful that Dash understood. "It sure can."

His gaze remained on her, and he didn't bother to hide his curiosity. "Do you mind if I ask what you do for a living? You said you're able to work at home."

"I own an online clothing boutique."

"I guess that explains the way you dress. Even when you were stuck in quicksand, you looked put together."

She glanced down at her shirt and shrugged. "I suppose. Who would I be if I didn't wear my own clothing?"

"That's great that you're able to do it online. But how are you even fulfilling any orders?"

"I have assistants at home who do that for me. I handle the marketing and some design."

"Well, I'm glad you're here and that our paths crossed."

Lizzie studied Dash another moment, getting that feeling again that she had seen him somewhere before.

"What?" Dash tilted his head under her scrutiny.

"I'm sorry. I don't mean to stare. It's just that there's something about you that just seems familiar. Which is crazy. I've never been to Cape Corral before so I have no reason that I would have ever seen you. I've never been to West Virginia either."

"That is weird," Dash said. "Maybe I have one of those faces."

His phone rang, and he glanced at the screen

before excusing himself and stepping toward the kitchen to answer.

As Lizzie watched him walk away, she realized why he looked familiar.

He bore a striking resemblance to someone she'd once read about in a magazine. A millionaire from New York City.

It was probably just a coincidence. After all, why would a millionaire be here in Cape Corral working as a saltwater cowboy?

CHAPTER SIXTEEN

"I'M WARNING YOU, don't let the deal go through. There will be consequences if you do."

The deep voice on the other end of the line made Dash's muscles tighten.

"Who is this?" Dash demanded.

"That's not important. You need to back off. We're on to you."

Dash's muscles bristled even more as he stepped farther away from Lizzie. "I have no intentions of backing off."

"That would be a mistake," the caller warned.

"Is that a threat? Do I need to remind you that I'm an officer of the law?"

"It's not a threat. It's reality." The phone line went dead.

Dash stared at his cell for a minute, still letting that conversation sink in.

Someone had obviously discovered he was buying up real estate here on the island. But how? Dash had been careful, taking every precaution so no one would connect him to the deals.

Yet, somehow, someone had found out.

Dash frowned as he put his phone away. He'd meant what he'd said. People could threaten him all they wanted. But what was done was done. Dash didn't intend on changing anything, no matter how unhappy his choices made some people.

Still, he often wondered how his friends would feel about this when they found out.

He knew he should tell them. But he didn't want anyone to know about his private life. If they did, their view of him would change. Not because they would mean for it to. But just because that was the way things happened.

Dash didn't want to be known for his past. He wanted to be known for who he was today. As much as he tried to tell himself that his background wouldn't matter to most people, in his experience, it did.

He put on his most relaxed smile as he walked back into the living room. He stopped in his tracks when he saw Lizzie sitting on the couch with her legs curled beneath her. She just looked so warm and cozy . . . and at home.

Like she belonged here.

Like she belonged with him.

Where were these thoughts coming from? They didn't make sense.

But the more Dash learned about Lizzie, the more affection he felt toward the woman. Knowing that she'd given up her own dreams to adopt her sister's child only solidified his feelings. It took a strong woman to take on that kind of sacrifice. But she'd been wise enough to also know the rewards.

Dash should squash these emotions before they got the best of him.

But he wasn't sure he wanted to.

———

"EVERYTHING OKAY?" Lizzie asked as Dash lowered himself beside her on the couch.

She'd barely heard him talking in the other room, but his words had sounded tense. Even now, his gaze appeared shadowed and a new tension stretched taut across his shoulders.

Dash nodded and released a long breath. "Just some business."

"People call you on a Sunday night because of business? Must be some job." She thought she was the only one who felt the need to be on call at all times. She was trying to break the habit, but it was hard. The whole work-life balance was trickier than all those self-help articles made it seem.

"It's a side business," he explained.

Lizzie thought again about how this man looked like the millionaire she'd read about. She couldn't remember the man's name. It hadn't seemed important at the time.

But she couldn't get the possible connection out of her mind.

The man she'd read about had been a hot commodity on the social scene. He'd not only been wealthy but single and handsome also. He was the kind of person the tabloids loved.

The mystery around Dash deepened—a mystery that Lizzie wouldn't mind solving.

"I should probably get you back to your house for some shut-eye," Dash announced. "I know it's been a long day for you and P-man."

Lizzie glanced out the window at the darkness outside and shuddered. She didn't mean to. But something about traveling to an empty house in the darkness had always made her nervous. Even when she lived in New York, she'd always tried to be home before it got too dark outside. The impulse was one of her crazy, irrational fears.

But that didn't change the shudder that went through her.

Despite her feelings, she knew that Dash's words were true. She should have probably gone home a couple of hours ago. They'd simply been having so much fun together . . . and the change had been nice. She hadn't realized how much she needed a day like today.

"I guess we should." Her gaze traveled to Preston as he snoozed on the loveseat.

"I hate to wake him," Dash said.

"Hate to wake him? Once he's sleeping, he's nearly impossible to wake." Lizzie stood. "Wait and see."

As she rose to her feet, Dash grabbed her hand and tugged her back down on the couch beside him.

Lizzie's heart pounded furiously in her chest as their gazes met. Was Dash thinking what she thought he was thinking?

She couldn't be sure. But she could hardly breathe as she waited to find out.

"It is awfully late," Dash said. "The two of you could just stay at my place if you want. No funny business. You could either have my guest bedroom or you could stay down here with your son. This is a pull-out couch."

"Don't you think people here in town would talk? I've never lived in a small town myself, but that's what I've always heard."

"I'm not too worried about what people will think. If anyone asks, I'll tell them it's none of their business, quite frankly."

"I would hate to tarnish your good boy reputation."

"There will be no reputation tarnishing here, I assure you." He smiled, a twinkle in his gaze.

The thought of staying here instead of returning home had its appeal. Not because Lizzie wanted to start anything with Dash or make him look bad. But she *was* exhausted. And she hadn't been lying when she said Preston was a bear to wake up. He weighed in at eighty pounds now, which made it impossible to carry him anymore, especially up the stairs at the beach house where she was staying.

"Maybe," Lizzie finally said.

"Maybe?" Dash raised an eyebrow.

"I don't like to make fast decisions."

He raised his hands in surrender. "I would hate to pressure you."

"That's good because I hate to be pressured."

His grin slowly faded. "Lizzie?"

"Yes?" Her breath caught when she saw the look in his eyes—it was downright mesmerizing.

"You are one of the most beautiful women I've ever met."

Lizzie's bones felt like they turned to mush. "Is that right? Maybe you don't get out enough."

He chuckled again. "There you go, deflecting the attention off yourself with some self-deprecation. I find that charming."

"I'm not trying to be charming."

"And that's the best part about it." He reached for her neck, his fingers entwining with her hair.

She didn't pull away. She didn't even think about it.

When he leaned toward her and their lips brushed, fire spread over her skin.

When the kiss deepened, Lizzie knew she never wanted it to end.

As they moved apart, she rested her head against the back of the couch, still facing Dash—still watching him, marveling over him, enjoying him.

She pulled a knee toward her chest, feeling

entirely too cozy. But she wouldn't complain. "I don't know what to say."

He still gazed at her, his hand resting on her leg. "You don't have to say anything."

"I didn't come here looking for romance you know."

"Neither did I." Dash leaned toward her again and pushed a stray hair behind her ear. "But I know when I see something good. And you, Lizzie McCreary, are something good."

Warmth rushed through her.

Before she could respond, Dash leaned forward and his lips met hers in another kiss.

CHAPTER SEVENTEEN

HE WATCHED them through the window. Most of the shades to the house were drawn, but the back window only had curtains.

He stood in the woods, in the shadows, where no one saw him.

Lizzie could not see him.

But he saw her.

His hands fisted at his sides. He didn't like what he watched.

Lizzie should be *his*. Always and forever.

Watching what unfolded was like watching a bad movie. He couldn't draw his eyes away.

But when he saw that man kiss Lizzie, anger boiled in his blood until he felt like he might explode.

He could *not* let this continue.

He had to think of a way to make Lizzie his. And Preston.

He kept watching, his eyes fastened to the scene.

"Get your hands off her," he growled. "Your lips too."

He stepped closer to the house. When he did, he saw the smile on Lizzie's face as she stared at the man sitting entirely too close to her.

She looked happy. How could she look happy?

She was only supposed to be happy with *him*.

A plan began to form in his head.

He would make sure that his message got through loud and clear. There would be no mistaking it. No more games. No more teasing.

Things had just risen to the next level.

Now he needed to get busy to set things into motion.

CHAPTER EIGHTEEN

DASH SMILED when he came downstairs the next morning and saw Lizzie sleeping peacefully on the couch.

His heart warmed at the sight of her. She was so beautiful, on the inside and out. He hadn't expected that kiss last night. But he didn't regret it either.

In fact, he looked forward to doing it again.

His smile widened.

He hoped.

Dash's footsteps hadn't awoken Lizzie, so he hurried into the kitchen. Maybe he would surprise her with breakfast.

But when his gaze went to the loveseat, Dash saw it was empty.

A moment of alarm rushed through him.

Where was Preston? Dash hadn't heard the boy moving around.

He scanned the room but didn't see anything out of place.

His suspicions continued to rise.

He hurried through the kitchen and glanced into the backyard. Maybe Preston had taken Goliath outside. He wouldn't put it past the boy.

But Dash's yard was also empty.

Just as he was about to step back into the living room, the bathroom door opened. Preston walked out with a big smile on his face, Goliath trailing behind him.

"Good morning," Preston whispered.

Relief filled Dash. "Good morning. You're up early."

"My mom always says the early bird gets the worm—although I don't know why anyone would want worms."

Dash glanced back at Lizzie again and saw she was still sleeping, despite their conversation. "Those sound like wise words, even if the worms don't make much sense."

Preston shrugged. "Maybe it's another fishing expression. Either way, my mom always has wise words, whether I want to hear them or not."

Dash walked into the kitchen and began to pull some pans from his cabinets. "Is that right? What other kind of wisdom does she give you?"

Preston climbed onto a bar stool and watched Dash as he worked. "Well, she says that who you date and marry is important."

That sounded about like something Lizzie would say—and she was absolutely correct. Dash pulled some eggs and bacon from the fridge, anxious to continue this conversation.

"Sounds smart. Anything else?"

Preston shrugged. "Can I help with breakfast?"

"Of course. Can you crack some eggs into that bowl?"

"I'm really good at that."

Dash smiled and set the carton in front of him, along with a bowl. "Then go ahead and do that. Let's surprise your mom with breakfast."

"She'll like that. Oh, she does say that image is important for us."

That was interesting. Lizzie didn't strike Dash as someone who was obsessed with status. But she did like stylish clothes. It only made sense since she owned a boutique.

Preston cracked some eggs into the bowl. As he

did, Dash grabbed a whisk and heated the oven so he could cook the bacon there.

"Your mom seems like a really special lady."

Preston nodded. "She says money can be a big deal."

Dash paused. Had he heard Preston correctly? Money was a big deal?

All the fears he'd had about any future relationships rose to the surface.

He'd seen something change on Lizzie's expression yesterday. She'd mentioned earlier that Dash looked familiar.

Had Lizzie figured out who he was? Was that the reason she'd warmed up to him so quickly last night?

Dash didn't want to think she was like all those other women he'd dated in the past—women who'd only liked him because he had money.

But what if Lizzie *was* like that? If she cared so much about image, about being careful who you dated and married, about money . . . what if she was interested in Dash only for what he could offer?

He tried so hard to keep that part of himself out of his life here.

But maybe it was impossible to escape.

LIZZIE AWOKE to the scent of bacon. To the sizzle of eggs. To the sound of happy voices talking in the kitchen.

As she pushed herself up on the couch, she remembered she was at Dash's. A smile stretched across her face as memories filled her.

Last night hadn't just been a dream. She and Dash really had kissed.

The warm fuzzy feelings she'd experienced were still there, dancing in her stomach.

Not only had they kissed, they'd discovered that there was something between them—something special.

Lizzie never imagined that coming to Cape Corral would be such a blessing.

Then again, she never expected to meet someone like Dash.

She stood from the couch and stretched before brushing her hair back from her face. She hoped she looked decent enough to see people. Since she hadn't brought anything here with her, her current look was going to have to work.

She stepped into the kitchen and saw Dash and Preston cooking together. The sight of it warmed her heart. Those two really did get along well—and that was an answer to prayer.

"Mom!" Preston abandoned his pan on the stove and bounced toward her, throwing his arms around her.

"Good morning, sweetie." She kissed the top of his head.

"We're fixing you breakfast," he announced.

Lizzie glanced at Dash and smiled. But the look Dash gave her wasn't quite as warm and bright as it had been yesterday.

"Good morning," he called before turning back to the pan in front of him.

What had changed? Or had Lizzie totally misread the situation?

Her stomach sank at the thought.

She didn't know. She, by no means, was an expert when it came to dating. In fact, she'd done so very little of it. Anyone she dated had to pass a test that mostly revolved around Preston. She'd been so busy raising the boy that she'd rarely taken time for herself.

Dash had checked off many of the boxes she'd mentally spelled out as essential qualities for someone she dated.

But maybe she'd been wrong—about everything.

About opening up. About how Dash felt. About her excitement over following her instincts.

A few minutes later, they all sat down to breakfast. Preston mostly dominated the conversation with his stories and questions and plans and adventures for the future.

Lizzie welcomed the change. She hardly even knew what to say, and the fact that she couldn't get a good read on the situation made her feel even more uncomfortable.

"I hate to cut this short, but I've got to get to work." Dash stood and picked up their plates.

"I can clean up," Lizzie insisted.

He waved her off. "I'll get it when I get back. It's no big deal. I'll drive you back to your house though. I'm sure the two of you have a lot to do today as well."

"I'd rather stay here." Preston's frown looked exaggerated.

"Too bad, buddy." Lizzie nudged his shoulder. "We've got schoolwork to do."

"Can I go pet Goliath one more time before we go?"

Lizzie glanced at Dash, who nodded.

"Why don't you do that real fast and then come back in?" she told him.

Preston sprinted outside, probably before anyone changed their minds.

When he was gone, Dash turned toward Lizzie. Based on the serious look in his eyes, this conversation wasn't going to be fun. She tried to brace herself for whatever was coming.

"I'm glad we have a moment alone." Dash shoved his hands into his pockets. "I wanted to talk about last night."

Lizzie wanted to gush, to say it had been wonderful. But she held back those words and waited, sensing something had changed. That wasn't the direction this conversation was heading.

"What's going on?"

"I shouldn't have kissed you." Dash rubbed his throat as he addressed her, apology emanating in his eyes. "I just got caught up in the moment and . . ."

"Don't worry about it," Lizzie rushed. "I was . . . I was totally thinking the same thing."

She forced herself to remain pleasant. Lizzie couldn't bring herself to reveal just how quickly she'd felt bonded with him. But there was no need to get that vulnerable with somebody who was essentially dumping her before they'd even started dating.

"Good." Dash offered a resolute nod, as if

surprised by how easy this conversation had been. "I'm glad you feel the same way. It was a bad idea."

"Exactly. I just need to concentrate on Preston and my job right now. So . . . let's just pretend like it never happened."

"That sounds great." Dash let out a deep breath, almost as if he was relieved to have that conversation over with. "Now, let's grab Preston and get you two back home."

CHAPTER NINETEEN

DASH FELT the tension between them as he drove Lizzie and Preston back to their cottage. But he was glad he'd said what he needed to say. The best thing he could do was to nip this relationship in the bud before it went too far.

But Dash would be lying if he said he wasn't disappointed.

He was almost even more disappointed when Lizzie seemed to accept his one-eighty so easily. Maybe part of him had hoped she would fight a little bit harder to give their relationship a chance. Maybe part of him wished that she would have denied that she knew who he was.

But Lizzie had seemed to accept the end of their relationship just as easily as he did. Not that Dash would have called it a *relationship*. But for him, what happened between him and Lizzie was the closest thing he'd had to a romantic relationship since he had come here to Cape Corral.

Thank goodness Preston filled the silence between them as the truck bounced along in the sand.

Dash was going to miss Preston. He hadn't known him long, but the boy had a way of worming his way into people's good graces. Dash had fun fishing with the boy yesterday. Listening to his tales. Seeing the excitement in his eyes.

But, Dash reminded himself again, this was for the best.

He glanced at Lizzie from the corner of his eye. She stared out the window, almost looking sad. Or was Dash just projecting the emotion on her?

Relationships were so much easier when they were shallow. But that wasn't what Dash wanted. Besides, things hadn't felt shallow between him and Lizzie. But he'd be a fool to jump into something too quickly.

Tension continued to tug across his chest.

Finally, Dash pulled up in front of Lizzie and Preston's house.

This was it. They would say goodbye, and Dash

would return to his life as it had been for the past three years. Lizzie, no doubt, would return to home-schooling and working. When the time came, she'd pack her bags and leave this place.

That thought made Dash much sadder than he'd thought it would.

But it was better to end this now than after he became too attached.

LIZZIE GRABBED THE DOOR HANDLE, wishing the ache in her chest would disappear. It was way too soon to feel this heartbroken. But that didn't change the fact that she did.

"Thanks again for everything," she muttered to Dash.

She was anxious to get out of the truck and have some space. The ride here had felt like torture and trying to hide how she really felt had drained her energy.

"Of course." Dash opened his door. "I'll walk you up."

"You don't have to—"

"I insist. I wouldn't be a cowboy if I didn't have

some manners." Dash tilted his hat, the twinkle in his eyes quickly disappearing.

Lizzie didn't want to smile, but she did anyway.

Preston skipped in circles around them as they walked toward the stairs.

Soon, this would all be over with. Dash would tell her goodbye. Most likely, Lizzie wouldn't see him again while she was here in town unless they ran into each other at church.

When she reached her door, she turned toward him, dreading this moment. What did she even say? She'd already thanked him for everything he'd done numerous times. She hated the awkwardness she felt.

Lizzie finally settled on, "I hope you have a great day at work."

Dash tilted his hat at her again, in that adorable way that she'd already come to love. "You too."

"What about those fish I caught?" Preston asked. "When are we going to cook them? You said we could."

Lizzie watched as a moment of distress washed over Dash's face. "We'll have to see if we can work that out, buddy. Two fish aren't quite enough for all three of us to eat."

"Then I can go fishing again and catch more."

Dash offered a sad smile. "I don't want to make any promises I can't keep. But we'll see, okay?"

Preston offered an exaggerated frown. "Okay."

With one more look Lizzie's way, Dash started down the stairs.

She turned to the door, punched in her code, and twisted the knob. But when the interior came into view, she saw that her whole house had been trashed.

CHAPTER TWENTY

BEFORE PULLING AWAY from the cottage, Dash looked back at Lizzie and Preston one more time. As he did, he saw Lizzie jerk backward. He saw the alarm on Preston's face.

Something was wrong.

Dash threw his truck back into Park then rushed up the stairs. As he peered through the doorway, he saw that the whole house had been turned upside down.

What...?

"Stay here," he ordered Lizzie.

Cautiously, Dash drew his gun and stepped into the house. He suspected that whoever had done this was long gone. But he needed to know for sure.

He glanced around again.

Whoever had done this had almost seemed angry. What other reason would this person have for turning couches upside down and tilting bookcases and smashing pictures?

Whatever had happened, Dash didn't like it.

He wasn't sure if he was speaking as someone who cared about Lizzie or a law enforcement professional. Probably both.

Dash checked the rest of the house, but no one was there. The place was clear.

Finally, he stepped back onto the deck where Lizzie and Preston waited for him. Lizzie hugged Preston as questions poured from the boy's mouth.

"Any idea who did this?" Dash locked his gaze onto Lizzie's.

Lizzie opened her mouth only to shut it again.

"Not anyone here . . ." she finally said.

The subtlety of her words wasn't lost on him. "But there's someone somewhere else?"

She glanced at Preston. The look on her face made it clear she didn't want to talk about the subject in front of her son.

Dash would wait—for now. But he was going to need more details if Lizzie wanted him to help keep her safe. In fact, she may not have a choice in this matter.

"I'm going to need to write up a report," Dash said. "Then you're going to pack your things."

Lizzie's eyebrows shot up. "What do you mean?"

"You're not staying here alone . . . not until we know what's going on."

"But—"

"No buts about it." Dash leveled his gaze with her. "You and I need to talk."

DESPITE HER RESISTANCE, Lizzie somehow found herself in the truck with Dash, Preston, and Gremlin two hours later.

Dash had taken pictures and filed a police report. He'd also collected fingerprints and looked for any shoe marks left outside. It was a long shot that they'd figure out who did this. Lizzie knew that.

Dash had called the local inn in town—run by Emmy—but Emmy had told him she was all full due to a fishing tournament in town this week. For that reason, Lizzie had no idea where Dash was taking her.

She'd packed up her things—she hadn't brought much—and the bags were in the back of the truck. Preston held Gremlin in his hands, occasionally petting the turtle's head.

Lizzie blanched when she pulled up to Dash's house again.

Anywhere but here. Please.

"I couldn't possibly impose," she started. It was her most polite argument at the moment, but soon she might turn desperate.

All she wanted was to get away from this man until she could gain control of her emotions.

Dash's jaw flexed. "It's the best place you can be until we know what's going on."

"But—"

"This is the only solution." Dash's voice sounded firm, leaving no room for argument.

"I think it will be fun, Mom." Preston looked at her with those wide eyes of his. "Maybe we can go fishing again and cook what we catch."

Lizzie opened her mouth to speak but closed it again. This didn't seem to be open for discussion. Part of her was comforted with the idea of staying here, especially when she remembered how unsettled she felt after seeing her house the way it was.

But if she stayed here, she was going to owe Dash

an explanation about what was going on. She really didn't want to get into her reasons for leaving New York.

But, as Preston and Dash climbed from the truck, it looked like she had no choice.

CHAPTER TWENTY-ONE

"YOU AND I NEED TO TALK," Dash told Lizzie as soon as they were inside his house.

She glanced at Preston again. "Sweetie, why don't you go in the backyard and check on Goliath? I'll be out in a few minutes."

Preston shrugged and skipped toward the back door, more than happy to have an excuse to play—and probably happy that his schoolwork routine had been interrupted.

When Lizzie glanced back at Dash, he saw the fire in her eyes. But Dash wasn't going to back down, no matter how angry Lizzie was with him.

His hands went to his hips. "You need to tell me what's really going on."

Lizzie crossed her arms. "Why should I tell you anything?"

"Because you're obviously in danger."

She raised her chin. "I can take care of myself."

"That's not the way it appears."

Her eyes narrowed even further as she lowered her voice. "I didn't ask you for your help."

"Nor do most people who are drowning. It's just obvious."

Lizzie shook her head and let out a laugh that sounded angry—if laughs could sound that way. "Here you go making it seem like I owe you my life story. The fact of the matter is, you've been hiding who you really are, not only from me but probably from most of the people on this island."

Dash's breath caught. Though he suspected that Lizzie knew, hearing her say the words out loud caused a temporary surge of panic to rush through him. "That's none of your business."

"Neither are my reasons for coming here. Why should I be expected to share everything while you're perfectly quiet about who you are and what brought you here?"

Dash knew he couldn't let his emotions get the best of him—and that's where this conversation was headed. "Look, we can stand here and argue and point fingers. Or we can try to figure out how to keep Preston safe. It's your choice."

He watched Lizzie's expression and saw it loosen. Finally, he had gotten through to her. This wasn't about their relationship—however quick it had been.

This was about Preston.

Lizzie looked to the side as if contemplating her thoughts.

And Dash waited for whatever she was about to say.

LIZZIE COULDN'T BELIEVE Dash's nerve.

Then again, she had to admit that he had a good point. As much as she wanted to be stubborn and wanted to let her hurt feelings get the best of her, that would prove nothing right now. She couldn't put her pride before Preston's safety.

"Do you want to sit?" Lizzie's throat burned as the words left her lips.

"Sure."

They stiffly lowered themselves across from each other on the couch. Before Lizzie started, she glanced back at Preston and saw him through the back window playing with the dog. He giggled and held a stick in the air as Goliath jumped to retrieve it.

Her smile disappeared as she turned back to Dash. She rubbed her hands on her jeans, wishing she could avoid this conversation.

But she no longer could.

She cleared her throat. "The truth is, I came here because I felt threatened."

"By who?"

"A man named Nicolai Rossi."

"And who is this Nicolai Rossi?"

"He's a man that I dated for a few months. He seemed nice enough at first, but, the more I got to know him, the more uncomfortable I became around him. I was especially concerned because he didn't seem to like Preston. He was always snapping at him and didn't have much patience. He never wanted to do things with the three of us together, just with him and me alone. I knew it wasn't going to work, so I broke things off."

"What happened then?"

"After that, I started feeling like I was being watched." Lizzie's voice trembled. "I felt like someone had been inside my house. Even when I was driving here, I felt like somebody was following me. I thought maybe I was being paranoid, though."

"Did you ever see Nicolai doing any of those things?"

Lizzie shook her head. "I didn't. He did call me a few times and even showed up at my place once, begging me to reconsider. I told him he needed to stop stalking me. He denied it, of course."

"So what led to you coming here?"

"Things went from bad to worse. I felt paranoid every time I left the house. I didn't want Preston going anywhere without me. It was affecting both of us. But the big, life-changing moment came when Preston and I were at an amusement park near where we lived and a man tried to grab Preston."

Dash's eyes widened. "What?"

Lizzie nodded, a sick feeling swirling in her gut as she remembered the events playing out. "I wish it wasn't true, but it was. Preston was waiting outside while I went into the restroom. We'd stopped at a place on the edge of the park—not one of the more popular areas. As Preston sat on the bench waiting for me, someone came up and told Preston he had to go with him."

"What did he do?"

"Preston refused. Of course. He told the man he

had to wait for his mom. But the guy insisted that Preston needed to go right then, that it was an emergency. Thankfully, I came out, and, when I did, the man ran away."

"Did you get a good look at him?"

"This is where it's probably going to sound a little crazy," Lizzie said. "He was dressed in character —like a chipmunk, actually. We didn't get a good look at his face. But it had to be Nicolai. He was the only one who made sense."

"But why would Nicolai try to grab Preston?"

"The only thing I can think of is that Nicolai wants to make things right, to make me think that he really does like Preston. I think he had some type of twisted plan of snatching him and keeping him until I realized that we could all be together."

"Did this guy show any signs of instability while you dated?"

Lizzie shrugged and released a long, drawn-out breath. "Maybe. Not at first. But he was pretty intense and pretty obsessive. He's not used to not getting his way. I knew I couldn't put Preston through that for any longer. Nicolai had turned our lives upside down."

"I'm going to need this guy's information so I can look into him."

"Of course. Like you said, whatever it takes to keep Preston safe."

When Lizzie glanced at Dash again, she could not help but lower her eyes. She was not going to enjoy this.

CHAPTER TWENTY-TWO

DASH HAD the unusual urge to open up to Lizzie.

But this wasn't the time or the place. He had more important things to do right now. Things like trying to find out if this Nicolai guy was on the island or not.

He didn't have any time to waste as far as he was concerned. But Dash also knew that he didn't want to leave these two at his house alone—not until he knew what was going on.

He stood. "How about if you two come with me to work? I can use my computer there to do some more searches. You'll be safe. You can even bring your computers and do your schoolwork and job stuff."

"If that's what we need to do." But Lizzie sounded resigned more than anything.

Dash hated the fact that she seemed resentful right now. He only wanted to protect her. But he knew things felt awkward since his rejection this morning.

He didn't have time to think about that now.

"We should get going," he said instead.

Ten minutes later, they arrived at the Community Safety building. Grant took Preston back to help him feed the horses while Lizzie set up her computer in the break room. Dash felt better having her here.

But he couldn't wait to dig in and find out a little bit more about this guy Nicolai.

He typed his name into the computer to see if there were any police reports on the man.

It looked like, when the guy was younger, he'd worked as a bouncer in a club up in New York. After that, he'd joined the military before getting out to become a consultant for a paramilitary agency. He'd had a small criminal infraction thrown out in court ten years ago after he'd gotten into an altercation outside a club.

Interesting. This man wasn't the kind of person he'd ever envisioned Lizzie with.

But Nicolai *did* look like the kind of guy who had a lot of money, which fit Dash's earlier assumption about Lizzie.

The woman valued image, status, and wealth.

Dash's heart sank with that thought. It was too bad. He'd really thought they might have something special together.

He needed to put in a few phone calls and see if he could figure out this man's whereabouts for the past week.

Dash needed answers.

For Preston's sake.

"HE WAS REALLY nice at first, you know." Lizzie leaned in the doorway and crossed her arms as she studied Dash's face.

He almost seemed startled to see her there.

"Nicolai?" Dash asked. "I'm sure he was."

But his words didn't sound convincing.

Lizzie had seen the doubt on his face. All the assumptions that he made.

A good girl wasn't supposed to go out with someone like Nicolai Rossi. But there was much more to that story.

"He'd supposedly turned his life around," Lizzie said. "He'd been a partier. A bad boy. He'd been in the military for a while, and he had plenty of tattoos to prove it. But when I met him, he had a respectable job as a consultant."

"Exactly how did you meet him?"

"At the gym. Which isn't my normal place to meet people. Honestly, I don't usually meet people at all. I've been quite content to be single, and he was the first guy that I gave a chance."

Dash's eyes showed he was thinking, processing, but Lizzie couldn't read exactly what was going through his mind.

"I'm sorry it didn't work out for you," he finally said.

"If it's meant to be, it's meant to be." Lizzie made sure to keep her voice firm. She believed those words. She wasn't going to compromise on what she wanted. And when she met a man who didn't like Preston or get along with him, then she obviously wasn't going to stay with him.

She had been entrusted with Preston's care, and she took that role very seriously.

"You're correct." Dash leaned back in his office chair and stretched his arms behind his head. "I made a few calls about him. No one's seen him in a week."

Lizzie's heart beat harder. She'd feared that's what he would say.

Maybe part of her had been hoping this was all a misunderstanding. Either way, she needed answers.

"I appreciate you doing this."

He shrugged. "It's my job."

Lizzie nodded. She had gotten Dash's message loud and clear. He wasn't doing this because he cared about her. He was doing this because it was his obligation.

And that was fine.

Because what was meant to be would be.

CHAPTER TWENTY-THREE

DASH PUT out an all-points bulletin to the other officers here on the island, as well as to the fire crew and those working for the town government. He included Nicolai's picture and a brief description of the man, making a point to say that their person of interest could be dangerous and that no one should confront him.

If Nicolai was on the island, Dash intended to find him.

Someone knocked at his door, and he turned to see Lizzie there.

"Sorry to interrupt you, but I realize that I left a couple of things at the house. It was hard to find everything I needed since the place was so strewn. Is there any way I could go back to grab these items? A couple things are for my work."

He nodded. "I can take you there."

"Great. Let me go grab Preston."

A few minutes later, the three of them were in his truck. As usual, it would have been a silent drive if it wasn't for Preston. The boy talked on and on about feeding the horses and even brought up the fact that he now wanted a horse himself.

The boy made Dash smile. In some ways, Preston actually reminded Dash a little bit of himself when he was younger. He'd always been driven, always had dreams, and he'd loved talking.

As Dash had gotten older, he'd realized that talking less got him into less trouble. It was a skill he had to work at.

"Look at that!" Preston exclaimed as he pointed to something in the distance. "That white bird with the long legs is standing on top of the tiny horse."

Dash smiled. "That's one of our newer foals here on the island. We call him Skeeter."

"Why is the bird sitting on him?"

"We like to call that bird a hitchhiker," Dash explained. "The bird—a cattle egret—eats the bugs the horses stir up. The horses don't seem to mind."

"I would," Preston said. "No free rides here."

"The birds also eat biting flies and ticks that irritate the horses, so it's a mutually beneficial relationship."

"That's good . . . I guess." Preston sounded uncertain.

Dash fought a smile as he pulled up to the house where Lizzie and Preston had been staying and put his truck in Park.

"Let me go in first," he said.

Lizzie and Preston nodded and climbed out of the truck to wait in the sand as Dash climbed the steps.

But just as Dash reached the deck, the door opened.

He reached for his gun and braced himself for a confrontation with whoever had been in this house.

***

AS LIZZIE STOOD outside near Dash's Bronco, she saw the door to her house opening. She pushed Preston behind her, worst-case scenarios rushing through her mind.

She fully expected Nicolai to emerge from her house, a gun in his hand and a stormy expression on his face.

Instead, a blonde woman with perky curls, appeared. A surprised expression captured her features, and her lips curled in a perfect O as she spotted Dash standing there.

"Mary Lou?" Dash's voice contained an edge of irritation. "What are you doing here?"

The woman's eyes widened. "I called Levi earlier, and he said I could come by to pick up something. You do remember that I work for the management company taking care of this house, right?"

Dash shook his head as if dumbfounded by the situation, and he put his gun away. "Yes, of course. I just wish I'd known you'd be here. I thought the person who did this had come back."

The woman's hand went over her heart as if frightened at the thought.

"I'm certainly glad you didn't point your gun at me. I was just trying to do my job." Her gaze fluttered to Lizzie, and her shoulders loosened just slightly. "Hi, there. You must be Ms. McCreary. Sorry about all this. I'll be sure to file an insurance report for the owner."

"I do hope that policy will cover this," Lizzie called up to the woman. "But if not, let me know. I'll make sure that this doesn't fall on the owner. They had nothing to do with this."

Dash and Mary Lou started down the steps toward them.

"Most renters we get aren't like that," Mary Lou said. "But I'll make sure the owners know that you said that."

Dash was still scowling, as if unable to shake off his irritation. "How is everything inside?"

"It's a mess." She shrugged. "Did you think otherwise?"

Dash's scowl grew deeper. "No, I didn't. But I wanted to check things out before I let Lizzie back inside."

"There's no one inside, if that's what you're asking."

Dash nodded at Lizzie, indicating that she and Preston could go up in a moment.

Lizzie would just hurry inside, grab what she needed, and be out of there. She had no desire to spend any more time in that house than necessary. Now, the place was associated with too many bad memories.

Though she wasn't looking forward to staying with Dash, another part of her was grateful she didn't have to stay alone either. Lizzie was certain she wouldn't have gotten any sleep if she had.

As she started toward the steps, Mary Lou's words stopped her cold.

"I just need to swing by and visit our other renter on this street," Mary Lou said. "I want to make sure he hasn't had any trouble."

Lizzie turned toward her. "I thought I was the only one staying on the street?"

Mary Lou shrugged, as if this wasn't a big deal. "Someone else checked in three days ago. I thought you knew."

"I haven't seen any cars outside." Lizzie had been keeping an eye on all the other houses, just to be safe.

"Oh, this guy doesn't have one. He said he likes to walk places. A lot of people do in this area."

Lizzie and Dash exchanged a glance.

"What did this guy look like?" Dash asked.

Mary Lou shrugged again. "I don't know. He was maybe thirty. Tall. Dark hair. Seemed like a city slicker."

"Did you get a name?"

"I think it was . . . Nick something."

Lizzie sucked in a breath. No . . .

Dash's jaw hardened. "I'm going to need you to let me inside that other house, Mary Lou. And I'm going to need for you to do that right now."

Lizzie knew exactly what he was getting at.

What if Nicolai had rented a house on this very street so he could keep an eye on Lizzie and Preston?

The very thought of it made her stomach squeeze and roil.

CHAPTER TWENTY-FOUR

"THE THREE OF you need to wait in my truck with the doors locked." Dash's voice left no room for argument. "Mary Lou, you need to tell me how to get into that house."

"Wouldn't it be easier if I showed you?" She blinked in confusion, as if this whole situation baffled her.

"I'm not sure who we're dealing with right now, so we need to be safe rather than sorry. I need you to give me that code."

Mary Lou's eyes widened, and she looked frazzled a moment before shaking it off and grabbing her phone. She punched in something before rattling off a string of six numbers. Dash added them in his phone. He waited until the three of them were safely in his truck with the doors locked before he strode down toward the house.

What if this Nicolai guy had been staying here this whole time?

He wouldn't put it past someone like Nicolai. At least, that was the impression Dash had of the man after talking to Lizzie. Dash had a hunch that this guy thought he was above the law and could do whatever he wanted to get what he wanted.

Dash needed to let him know that wasn't going to fly here in Cape Corral.

He picked up his phone and called for some backup, just in case things turned ugly.

Levi pulled up just a few minutes later. He threw his Jeep in Park before meeting Dash. The two of them strode toward the front door together. As per protocol, they knocked first and identified themselves.

When no one answered, Dash entered the code Mary Lou had given him. Since this man didn't own the house, Dash and Levi could go inside without a warrant.

The interior looked like most of the other houses here in this area that had been built forty years ago. Dark wood paneling, low ceilings, and grungy carpet greeted them.

Dash glanced around, praying he didn't run into trouble here.

But some answers would be really nice.

They searched the living room but saw nothing. Almost like no one had been here.

The kitchen was the same except for some milk and bread left in the refrigerator.

Someone had been here recently. The milk hadn't expired.

Levi motioned to Dash as he headed toward the bedrooms. Dash nodded and followed behind, still on guard. Situations like this demanded caution. The last thing they wanted was to be ambushed.

The first bedroom was empty.

So was the second.

But the third bedroom showed that someone had been here recently. The bed sheets were rumpled and a few clothing items were on the dresser.

Nobody was there now.

Levi paused beside a desk in the corner and glanced at something left there.

"You're going to want to see this," he said.

LIZZIE COULD HARDLY BREATHE AS she waited for Dash and Levi to emerge from the house.

Time seemed to slow as apprehension crawled through her muscles.

Meanwhile, Mary Lou chattered beside her. Lizzie had thought Preston talked a lot, but Mary Lou might beat him in a competition. The woman went on and on about the great housing market in this area, the worry that many locals had over the land being bought up, and how she was about to enter a cake contest that the community was known for.

Lizzie only half listened.

Instead, she waited, praying that nothing happened to the two men who'd gone inside.

Could it be true? Could Nicolai have been staying two houses down from Lizzie, all while she'd been clueless?

She thought she'd been so smart, so clever when she'd come here. Not only that—she'd also thought she'd covered all her tracks.

But, again, the Lord had humbled her. Lizzie was beginning to realize more and more that she could *not* do this by herself.

Finally, Dash stepped outside and motioned to Lizzie. She opened her door and climbed out.

"Can you come up here for a second?" he yelled across the space between them.

"What about us?" Mary Lou called. "Do I have to stay in here?"

"You can get out, but stay close."

With a touch of trepidation, Lizzie trudged across the sandy landscape before climbing the steps to the deck where Dash waited for her. He held something in his gloved hands.

Did she really want to know what?

He put some papers on a picnic table, and her eyes caught sight of the images there.

Photo paper, Lizzie realized. Dash found pictures inside.

She stepped closer, wanting a better look at them. But what she saw caused her to suck in a deep breath.

They were photos of her.

And Preston.

All taken while here on Cape Corral.

Any of the lies Lizzie had wanted to tell herself about the person behind these incidents disappeared. She was clearly the target.

Somebody—most likely Nicolai—had been watching her every move.

All the feelings Lizzie had experienced, feelings

that she was being watched, weren't her being crazy or overreacting.

Someone really *had* been stalking her and Preston.

Maybe even at that fishing hole when she'd been with Dash and Preston, when she'd heard the sound of a stick cracking in the woods.

She shivered.

"You okay?" Dash's voice pulled her from her panicked thoughts.

"Not really," Lizzie answered. "I can't stay here. I need to find somewhere else to go. Somewhere safe."

She rubbed her temples as she felt an ache beginning there.

She needed to find somewhere Nicolai couldn't locate her. But if not Cape Corral, then where? Lizzie had been so certain that this was her best option.

Dash gripped her arm. She tried not to flinch at his touch and the warmth it brought with it.

"You should stay," he murmured, as if reading her thoughts.

"But he knows I'm here. He's watching me. He's coming after me. What possible good could come from me staying here?"

He leveled his gaze with her. "At least when you're here, you have people to watch out for you."

Lizzie let Dash's words sink in. His assurance brought her an unusual comfort. Even though the man had rejected her this morning, he obviously cared about doing his job on the island. He cared about keeping residents and visitors safe.

She glanced back down at Preston as he swung himself around a pole outside. That boy was her whole world. "I've got to keep him safe."

"I can help you with that."

Lizzie's gaze snapped back to Dash's. "You have other cases to work. You have horses to tend. You don't need to be babysitting me."

Dash stepped a little closer—close enough that Lizzie felt her cheeks heat. She wished the man didn't have that effect on her. But that didn't change the reality that he did.

"I don't mind." His voice sounded husky, and his gaze appeared almost smoky as he stared down at her.

Lizzie wanted to argue. She really did.

But she had no other ideas. If she left here, she didn't know where she would go or how she would get there.

So, for now, she'd stay. At least until she figured out something else.

She'd be wise to keep Dash's rejection at the forefront of her mind.

But when he looked at her like he did now and spoke with that low, rumbling voice . . . all she wanted to do was forget.

Forgetting wasn't something her heart could handle.

CHAPTER TWENTY-FIVE

WHILE LEVI WORKED THE SCENE, Dash drove Mary Lou to her car, which she'd left at the top of the dune. Some people didn't prefer driving down this street because it was too difficult to climb the dune back up to the main road cutting through town.

Mary Lou was obviously one of them.

He dropped her off, she thanked him, and then Dash, Preston, and Lizzie headed away from the rental.

He was going to take them to The Screen Porch Café. Preston had said he was hungry earlier. They had blown through lunchtime, staving off their hunger with some crackers and soda from the machine down at the station. But Dash knew that wasn't enough to sustain them for long.

Plus, Dash could see that both Lizzie and Preston probably needed a mental break from everything that had happened. Especially Preston. Dash didn't want the boy to worry too much.

Preston glanced around at the screened porch turned restaurant. "This place is cool."

Dash smiled. "We like it here. It's home cooking at its finest."

"My mom's idea of home cooking is reheating takeout."

"Preston!" Lizzie's eyes widened as she looked at her son.

He shrugged. "What? It's true. You said we should always be honest."

"I can cook a few things," she offered feebly. "But takeout is so easy."

After they were seated, Dash was careful to keep the conversation light. He didn't want to do anything to concern Preston.

But it was hard to ignore the fact that Lizzie seemed unusually quiet. Obviously, she had a lot on her mind.

Instead, Dash told Preston about the wild horses,

about the new foals that had been born, about how the stallions fought over mares.

After their food was delivered and they'd prayed, Dash quickly checked the messages on his phone. Nobody had stepped forward to say they could identify Nicolai or that they'd seen him here on the island.

Dash fought a frown. If this man was here, he could only stay hidden for so long. The island had eight thousand acres, but much of it was wooded. Eventually, this Nicolai guy would need to get food and water. He would need a place to stay at night, especially since he probably knew, at this point, that his rental was under surveillance.

They *were* going to find this guy, Dash vowed. It was just going to take some time.

"This fried fish is really good." Preston licked some tartar sauce from his lips.

Dash grinned "It is, isn't it? I wouldn't lie to you."

Meanwhile, Lizzie barely nibbled away on her shrimp taco salad.

Despite Dash's resolve to keep her at a distance, he had to admit his heart went out to the woman. Part of him wanted to reach out, to try to offer her some comfort.

Another part of him wanted to feel her lips

against his. Wanted to inhale her coconut and vanilla scent.

But Dash reminded himself that would be a bad idea.

The best thing he could do right now was to concentrate on keeping Lizzie and her son safe.

LIZZIE WAS thankful that Dash wanted to go back to his house after dinner. She was exhausted and some time out of the spotlight sounded good, even if that did mean time alone with Dash.

He'd told her that Levi was actively investigating the man who'd been staying at the house two doors down. Meanwhile, Dash had brought his computer home so he could work there.

As soon as they got inside, Preston ran off to the back porch to play with Goliath. They'd have to double up on schoolwork tomorrow. Preston's attention span was pretty much shot for the day.

Lizzie grabbed her own computer. The distraction would be nice for now. It certainly beat talking to Dash.

But she found it difficult to concentrate on what she needed to do. She tried to focus on some more menial tasks that didn't require as much concentration or creativity by responding to some social media comments, approving some designs, and doing a quick cost benefit analysis for a new clothing line.

Lizzie *did* love her job. She'd started this business with nothing except an idea and a dream. She'd never expected it to grow as it had. The first year that she had made enough with the business to support herself and to buy a house, Lizzie felt like she was walking in the clouds.

But with her own business also came challenges. Work-life balance could be hard. Managing people had its difficulties. Having to fire those who didn't meet her standards made her sleepless.

As she finished her tasks, she closed her laptop and let her head rest back against the couch. Preston and Goliath were still playing, and she was so grateful her son liked to entertain himself. Otherwise, this single mom gig would have been much harder.

She loved listening to Preston's laughter as he played ball with the dog in the backyard. Apparently, dogs were a little more exciting than box turtles.

Before she could delight in the scene for too long, a knock sounded. Lizzie stared at the front door, contemplating whether or not she should answer.

Dash appeared from the downstairs bedroom where he'd been working. He motioned for her to stay put as he went to answer.

But before he reached it, gunfire rang through the air.

The wood on the front door split as a bullet pierced it.

And Dash dropped to the floor.

CHAPTER TWENTY-SIX

"GET DOWN!" Dash yelled as he crouched low.

More bullets exploded through the air, sending splinters and dust all over him.

What was going on out there?

He knew.

Someone wanted to send a clear message.

Maybe even to kill.

Dash's heart pounded into his ribcage at the thought.

Finally, the barrage stopped.

Dash looked up, the acidic smell of gunfire turning his stomach.

Lizzie cowered behind the couch, her body turned toward the backyard.

Where Preston was.

The boy should be okay. The bullets hadn't gone that far.

But Dash needed to make sure.

"Preston . . ." Lizzie muttered, her voice stretched thin with desperation.

"Stay there! I'll check on him."

Dash darted toward the back porch and saw the boy hunkering behind a wall, squeezing Goliath. He appeared frozen with fear—but otherwise unharmed.

"You okay, buddy?" Dash leaned toward him.

The boy nodded, his eyes still wide and dazed.

"Go inside with your mom."

Preston shot to his feet and ran through the door.

As he did, Dash hurried back into the living room, nearly colliding with Lizzie as she rushed toward Preston.

"I need to go find this guy," he rushed, knowing there was no time to waste. "You two go in my room and lock the door. Now."

Lizzie nodded, already racing toward his bedroom with Preston in tow. "Got it! Now go! We're fine."

Once he knew they were safe, Dash sprinted outside.

Whoever had fired those bullets was gone.

Had this person been driving?

Had the shooter gotten out of the vehicle long enough to knock before hopping back into his truck to fire? The man could have pulled away after his shooting spree.

Dash pulled his keys from his pocket and jumped into his truck. As he took off down the road, he called Levi and told him what had happened.

His friend was headed this way.

Dash continued through the island, searching for any sign of the gunman.

But the sandy road ahead was clear.

He searched side streets and nearby driveways for signs of trouble.

Nothing.

How had this guy gotten away so quickly? It didn't make sense.

Dash wasn't giving up yet.

He did another sweep of the area. He passed several people outside near their vehicles. But they were all locals, all people he knew. He asked them if they'd seen anything, but no one had.

There was only one other place he could try.

The beach.

He turned his wheel that way.

When he pulled onto the sandy shore, he saw

that the tide was especially high today. It would be nearly impossible to drive on the small shoreline right now.

He hit his hand on the steering wheel, trying to control his frustration.

The shooter had gotten away.

But that didn't mean Dash was giving up.

"IT'S GOING TO BE OKAY," Lizzie murmured.

She sat on the floor, her back against the bed behind her, as Preston leaned into her arms. His thick, blond hair felt sweaty, and a sheen of perspiration scattered across his sun-kissed skin.

She desperately wanted to comfort her son. But she could sense he was still upset. Who wouldn't be after what had just happened?

Lizzie could barely contain the tremble that rushed through her bones.

Dash could have died back there.

That was what the shooter wanted, wasn't it? He'd knocked, hoping that someone would be on the other side when he shot at the door.

What if Preston had answered?

Her trembles deepened.

She prayed Dash would catch the person responsible.

Please, protect him. Protect us.

Her requests felt endless.

Nicolai's picture rushed through her mind. How could he do something like this? Lizzie had no idea when she met him that he'd be so awful. If so, she would have stayed far away.

But the man had seemed so charming. He'd been attentive. Complimentary. When she was too busy for a night on the town, he'd offered to go grocery shopping with her instead.

Lizzie had fallen for him . . . hook, line, and sinker.

She held back a groan. Now that she'd started with the fishing expressions, she couldn't seem to stop herself.

"Do you think Dash is okay?" Preston mumbled into her shoulder.

"I think so, honey." She prayed he was.

"I like him, Mom." Preston pulled back just enough to look at her.

"He's a nice man."

"I mean, I really like him."

Lizzie's heart pounded in her ears when she heard the serious tone of his voice. "I like him too,

Preston. But don't get too close. I don't know how long we'll be here."

"I don't want to leave, Mom." Preston's gaze latched onto hers, leaving no doubt that he meant the words. He really liked Cape Corral, even with everything that had happened since they arrived.

Lizzie rubbed his back and tried to find the right words. "Sweetie . . . I'm glad you like it here. But we have our place back in New York."

"This is better."

"Oh, honey . . ." She wanted him to be happy. But at what cost? She wasn't sure of the answer to that question. Life was rarely as simple as spiffy sayings seemed to indicate.

"You don't even like New York."

"I know. But could you really see yourself here all the time?" When Lizzie had come to Cape Corral, she never thought she'd have this conversation with her son. Staying here hadn't even been on the table. She'd just assumed Nicolai would eventually go away and life would resume.

But that thought had been foolish, hadn't it?

"I can see myself here," Preston said. "I want to help with horses and catch fish and eat fried chicken with people after church."

Lizzie nodded, unsure what else to say.

Instead, she paused as the front door opened.

Footsteps pounded across the floor.

Lizzie braced herself.

Who was here?

Dash? Or the bad guy?

CHAPTER TWENTY-SEVEN

AS DASH STEPPED into the house, he noticed how incredibly quiet it was. His boots clunked across the hardwood floor as he strode toward his room and knocked at the door.

"Lizzie? Preston? You guys still in there?"

A moment later, he heard Goliath bark. The door flew open. Lizzie and Preston stood there, both of their eyes wide and uncertain.

Dash raised his hands, trying not to alarm them. "It's just me."

"Did you catch him?" Lizzie rushed, her hopeful eyes latched onto his.

He shook his head, regretting his answer. "I wish I could tell you yes. But he somehow managed to get away. My guys are out there looking for him now and asking if anybody saw anything."

Lizzie swallowed so hard that her throat visibly tightened. "I hope you can catch him. I'm . . . sorry."

"There's nothing to be sorry about. You didn't know any of this would happen."

Lizzie pulled Preston tighter as she glanced at Dash. "I'm glad you're okay."

"I'm glad you're all okay also. I need to board up the front door and write a report about what happened here tonight though. Can you two entertain yourselves for a while?"

Lizzie nodded. "Of course. We'll just be in here playing a game of Uno until you're ready for us to come out."

Dash nodded, wishing there was more he could do for them now. He wished he could pull Lizzie into his arms and tell her that everything was going to be okay.

But he couldn't do that. It pained him to keep his distance.

How many times was he going to have to have this same conversation with himself?

TWO HOURS LATER, Dash's colleagues left. A board had been nailed over his door where the four bullets had been fired into it. The splinters had been swept up. The bullets had been collected as evidence. The few little knickknacks that had been broken were put into a trash bag and placed in the can outside.

Everything still seemed so unreal to Lizzie, like this was something that happened to other people but not to her.

But it *was* happening to her, whether she liked it or not.

Relief filled her when Preston went up to the guest bedroom to go to sleep. Goliath had gone with him, and Dash had given permission for the dog to sleep beside him on the bed. Preston was thrilled.

But now Lizzie hoped that she and Dash would have a chance to talk.

As soon as she came back downstairs from tucking Preston in, Dash turned toward her. Lizzie could see in his eyes that he wanted to talk also.

But she would start first.

"You could have died." Her voice cracked as she said the words.

"Thankfully, everyone is okay."

"It could have turned out so much differently."

"Lizzie . . ." He said her name so softly that warmth rushed through her.

She wasn't sure how it happened. But, in the next instant, she was in his arms. Not romantically. Not really. That's what Lizzie told herself, at least.

But she'd been trying so hard all day to be strong for Preston. Now it was nice to have someone be strong for her.

Not that Lizzie should get used to this.

Dash had been a jerk earlier. Kissing her one moment and telling her they had no future together the next. She had no idea what was going through his mind.

But, right now, Lizzie was grateful for his strong arms. For his leathery aftershave. For his soothing words.

"Can we sit down for a second?" Dash asked.

"Of course."

He kept a hand on her arm as he led Lizzie over to the couch. They sat beside each other, a respectable distance apart.

"I've been thinking about what you said earlier," he said. "About how you've opened up to me and told me about your life, but I've been pretty quiet about my own."

Lizzie shook her head. She shouldn't have said

that. She'd been speaking out of anger. "It's okay, Dash. I wasn't myself."

"No, I want to say something. I *need* to say something."

She shrugged, curious now about what Dash had on his mind. She waited for him to start.

"I was telling you the truth when I said I grew up in West Virginia," he said. "My mom and I worked for Thomas Armstead. He owned a huge horse farm. We were basically stable workers. My dad left when I was young, and this job offered housing for my mom and me."

"Explains your love of horses," Lizzie said.

"My mom and Thomas eventually fell in love and married," Dash continued. "Thomas had wanted to expand his businesses by starting a perfume and beauty line. He asked my mom to head it up. She was a good businesswoman and had even done some work in fashion before I was born."

Lizzie nodded and waited for him to reveal the rest of his story.

"You may have heard of her. Lauren Fulton. Her perfumes are available at high-end department stores across the country."

Lizzie's eyes widened. "Your mom is Lauren Fulton?"

Lauren Fulton had practically become a household name over the past decade. Her perfumes were exquisite.

"The one and only," Dash said. "You really didn't know?"

"I thought you might seem familiar, but I had no idea."

Dash nodded slowly before continuing. "After college, I moved to New York and worked for her. I came to Cape Corral to do some research for some colognes I was considering launching as a part of my own company. That's when I fell in love with this area. I actually ended up branding some of the scents as Back in the Saddle, Cowboy Up, and Campfire Cowboy."

"I've smelled some of those. They're great." They really were. Lizzie loved the leathery scents—and so did thousands of others. The manly aromas had been a huge hit.

"I never expected to have that kind of success on my own. To be truthful, it was overwhelming. The thing was . . . after a while, I felt like everyone wanted a piece of me."

"What do you mean?" She waited for him to continue, more than curious about this part of his life. She'd had no clue.

"It suddenly felt very unclear who liked me for me, and who liked me for what I could do for them." He pressed his lips together as if a war raged inside him.

"Did something happen to make you feel that way?"

As Dash's face darkened, Lizzie knew she'd struck a nerve. She waited to hear what he had to say.

CHAPTER TWENTY-EIGHT

DASH WIPED his hands on his jeans, surprised at how nervous he was.

But he hadn't shared his story with anyone since he came here. Why was he sharing these details with Lizzie now?

Maybe it was because he felt she could understand. She was new here. And there was something about her, something about the look in her eyes, that made him feel they had a connection—an unusual one at that.

"I thought finding my own success was what I wanted," he continued. "And, for a while, it was. I loved feeling like I'd achieved something on my own. I even liked the events that went with being in that world. But with that came challenges. Honestly, I didn't even like the crowd I was hanging with."

Lizzie folded her arms over her chest. "So how did you become a law enforcement officer here?"

He sighed and ran a hand through his hair. "I couldn't forget about my visit to this area. On a whim, I applied to work for the Forestry Division here. I didn't think I'd get in or even be considered, especially with my background."

"You told them you own a cologne company?" Her eyes fastened on him, as if totally absorbed with his story.

"I actually left that part out, but I was sure to include my master's degree in business and marketing. I'd worked with horses, so I think that counted in my favor."

"And you got the job?"

Dash shrugged. "It wasn't quite that easy. I had to go through an academy for training. I wasn't even sure I would be placed here. I had no idea what would happen."

"Meanwhile, you gave up your career, not knowing what the outcome would be?"

Those days flashed through his mind, as vivid as if they'd happened yesterday. "I did. I hired a CEO to manage operations for me, but I'm still the primary stakeholder in the company. Any big decisions need to come through me. I'm pretty hands off, otherwise."

"That was a huge leap." Admiration stretched through Lizzie's voice.

Dash nodded. "It was. I still shake my head, wondering what I was thinking at times. But I wouldn't change it for the world. I've learned so much since I've been here. I love the beach, the ocean, the slower-paced lifestyle. And I really love the horses. It's like I'm living my boyhood dream of being a cowboy."

"City slicker turned cowboy." Lizzie smiled and shook her head as if in slight disbelief. "That's quite a story."

"I don't tell many people. I actually like to keep my past private. It's easier that way. As soon as people think you have money . . ." His voice trailed. It sounded like a strange burden, but, in some ways, it was just that. Most people didn't understand. They thought money solved all problems.

It didn't.

"People treat you differently," Lizzie finished. She almost sounded like she understood.

"Exactly."

"I'm sure that can be difficult."

"It is. I never talk about this."

She tilted her head, sincerity seeming to beam from her gaze. "Thank you for trusting me, Dash. That means a lot."

"I just wanted you to know that you're not the only one dealing with problems. I've got some of my own."

Lizzie glanced at the door that had been battered with bullet holes and bandaged with plywood. "I'd say we both do."

AS LIZZIE LAY in the guest bedroom, sleep wouldn't find her.

The room contained two twin beds. Preston slept in one, and she lay in the other. Goliath stretched out beside her son.

Meanwhile, Dash slept downstairs. Although, knowing him, Lizzie would guess he wasn't getting much sleep tonight either. Not after what had happened earlier.

She shivered as she remembered those bullets piercing his front door. She couldn't stop thinking about the what ifs.

What if Preston had answered? What if it had

been her—and Preston was left without anyone? What if Dash had died? If so, there would be no one to blame but Lizzie.

She pulled her blankets higher.

Coming to Cape Corral had been a bad idea. But where else could she go? Where would she be safe? Or would Nicolai just keep finding her? Keep following her?

How *had* he found her here, for that matter?

She'd been so careful. Although she'd felt as if she was being followed as she'd driven here, she had made certain no one had actually followed her.

Lizzie had ditched her old cell phone for a new one.

She'd only paid using cash.

No one in the office even knew her exact location.

She frowned and turned over, hating how unsettled she felt.

Her thoughts went to Dash and what he'd told her tonight.

He was Jason Fulton.

A millionaire had moved here to Cape Corral, and no one even knew it.

She let out a quiet chuckle at the thought.

Dash lived so humbly. It was no wonder that no one had guessed who he really was.

It certainly made the man even more fascinating.

However, Lizzie suspected he was still hiding secrets. But what else?

She didn't know. She had other things to worry about right now.

Things like where she could go when it came time for her to leave here and find another hiding spot.

CHAPTER TWENTY-NINE

DASH DECIDED to surprise Lizzie with breakfast one more time.

Last time, it hadn't ended well.

Preston had told Dash a little more than he'd really wanted to know about Lizzie.

Dash had withdrawn.

Now he wondered if that was a mistake.

Because Dash's gut told him that Lizzie wasn't like the other women he'd dated. She didn't seem to care about money or social position. Why was he so gun-shy on these issues?

He knew.

Because of Isabell.

Isabell Florence had swept into his life and stolen his heart. He'd seen forever with her. But when he'd mentioned giving everything up and coming to Cape Corral for a simpler life, she'd scoffed.

Throughout the following months, it had become clear to him that Isabell only liked wealthy Dash. She didn't like simple-life Dash.

Which meant that their relationship was never really about a mutual attraction for each other.

It had been about Dash's money. Isabell had never held a job for long. She had expensive tastes. She was never thankful for anything Dash did for her.

The signs were all there. He'd just been too infatuated to see them.

Dash sighed and flipped a pancake.

As he did, Preston and Goliath appeared in the doorway. Preston rubbed his eyes, which still drooped with sleepiness.

"Good morning," Dash called.

As Goliath barked, Preston opened the door to let him outside. "Morning."

"Your mom still sleeping?"

Preston nodded and climbed onto a bar stool to watch Dash cook. "She is. But she hardly ever sleeps past seven, so she should be up any time now."

"I see."

"Sometimes, when we take vacations, she sleeps in. That's about the only time."

Interesting. Preston was much more of an open book than Lizzie was. And Dash had to admit that he was curious. As closed as he'd been about his own life, he knew he had no right to want to know more about Lizzie.

Maybe he shouldn't ask, but he found the question leaving his lips anyway. "Do you guys take a lot of vacations?"

Preston shrugged. "Usually just to our beach house."

Surprise washed through Dash. "Your beach house?"

"My mom says she likes to go there to get away and clear her head. I think it's boring—unless I can bring a friend with me. Then it's fun."

"What else does your mom do for fun?"

Preston shrugged. "She likes to go to the health club."

"The health club? Is that like the gym?"

Preston shrugged again. "I just know that's what she calls it."

Before Dash could ask any more questions, Lizzie appeared at the base of the stairs. She'd already dressed for the day.

Seeing her took Dash's breath away.

He *had* to stop reacting like that to her.

But the woman fascinated him.

All the promises he'd made to himself didn't change that.

"I thought I heard you guys talking down here." Lizzie slid onto the bar seat next to Preston and gave him a quick side hug.

"I thought you were sleeping." Dash flipped another pancake.

"I had trouble falling asleep last night, actually." She frowned and stared out the window, as if looking for more trouble.

Dash had also had trouble sleeping. He couldn't stop thinking about the gunshots that had been fired through his door. He was determined to catch whoever had done that.

But he was also determined to keep Lizzie and Preston safe.

Doing both would be a challenge.

His phone rang, and Dash tensed when he saw the number.

"I need to take this," he told Lizzie.

She walked around the breakfast bar to the griddle. "It's fine. I'll finish these up. I don't mind."

Reluctantly, he stepped back and handed her the spatula. "Thank you."

He dreaded hearing what Clarkson had to say this time.

———

WHAT WAS the phone call about? Lizzie couldn't help but wonder as she finished cooking the pancakes.

By the time Dash was back inside, she'd used up the batter and set a plate stacked high with the hotcakes on the breakfast bar.

"All done," she announced. "Hope they measure up to yours."

"I'm sure they will." Based on Dash's shadowed expression, the call hadn't been a good one.

Instead of talking about it, Dash grabbed some fruit salad from the refrigerator and carried it to the table. He'd already set the plates and syrup out, so everything was ready to go.

As they sat down together, Lizzie couldn't help but muse at how natural this felt. Despite Dash's rejection, there had been something between them. She was certain Dash couldn't deny that fact either.

But she couldn't get used to doing this or to staying here.

Dash had made it clear that, despite their chemistry, they had no future together.

Her heart clenched as she remembered the conversation.

"So you have some schoolwork to do today, don't you?" Dash asked Preston, pulling Lizzie from her thoughts.

Preston frowned and paused from pouring syrup on his pancakes. "I guess."

"Yes, you do," Lizzie corrected.

Preston shrugged and stabbed a piece of his pancake, syrup dripping from his fork as he raised it to his mouth.

Lizzie glanced at Dash. "I know you have work to do too. Don't feel like you need to keep an eye on us."

Dash's expression tightened. No doubt he was thinking about that gunfire from yesterday. They all were. How could they not?

"I was wondering if you guys might want to come to the station with me and work there. Someone will be there at all times, so you'll be safe."

Lizzie nodded, not wanting Dash to rearrange

his schedule for her. The compromise seemed reasonable. "That will be fine."

"Can I feed the horses again?" Preston's eyes lit with excitement.

Dash smiled. "I'm sure that we can arrange something."

Before they could talk more, Dash's phone rang again. This time he answered at the table. But after saying a few things into the mouthpiece, he ended the call and looked at them.

"A brawl has started on the other end of the island. It's all hands on deck. Sorry to cut this breakfast short, but I need you guys to grab your things and go with me."

CHAPTER THIRTY

DASH GRIPPED the steering wheel as he headed down the road. He didn't like what was happening here on the island. Not at all.

That first call had been from his lawyer. Things with the property deals were escalating, and more angry emails had come into his business office.

Not Dash's cologne business, but another LLC he'd set up. Dash had done so purposefully so people couldn't connect him to this company. Some aspects of his life, he liked to keep quiet.

But everything was beginning to blow up. What had started as something he hadn't wanted attention for had turned into something largely misunderstood.

"So where are we going?" Lizzie asked beside him.

His scowl deepened as he stared out the front window. The last thing Dash wanted was for Lizzie to experience this. The island—ordinarily—was great. Things had been turned upside down over the past few months, however.

The island harbored some ugly truths that Lizzie wouldn't be able to avoid.

"You know that land I told you about that's being bought up on the island?" he started.

"I remember."

"Locals think that a family—the Fergusons—have been purchasing it. And they *have* been buying up some of the land. In fact, an easement is one of the only things stopping them from building on some of the property they procured. Dani owns it—and she's not selling."

"Then what's the problem?"

"Some of the locals aren't very happy about these changes, so they organized a protest outside the Fergusons' house. The Fergusons called the police, and a fist fight broke out between certain members of the community and the Fergusons. Levi and Grant are there now trying to control the situation. They need me out there to help."

Lizzie released a soft breath. "It's hard to believe that such a peaceful little island can have so many problems."

His jaw tightened. "Isn't it, though?"

Dash spotted a crowd standing in front of an oversized beach house in the distance and slowed.

More people were here than he'd imagined. Probably thirty people had shown up for the protest.

Dash threw his vehicle in Park and turned to Lizzie. "I need you to stay here. If you have any trouble, lay on this horn and I'll be here in five seconds flat. Okay?"

Lizzie nodded, but he couldn't help but notice how pale her face was.

He would keep an eye on his truck as he worked this scene.

But right now, he felt like he was being pulled in too many directions. All he really wanted was to focus—to give all his attention to Lizzie and Preston.

Maybe once he got control of this situation, he'd be able to do just that.

"WHAT'S GOING ON UP THERE, Mom?" Preston looked up at her as they sat in the front seat of Dash's truck.

Lizzie's eyes were fastened on the scene playing out in the distance. "Some people are having a disagreement."

"By fighting? Shouldn't adults know better by now?"

Lizzie shook her head. "Good point. But they're only fighting with their words—at the moment, at least."

She could tell by the body language of some people that they were only seconds away from being triggered—before things turned violent.

Dash wandered among the crowd, talking to several people. His hand rested at his hip, almost like he wanted to display his badge and remind people that more law enforcement had arrived. The man had a good presence for these kinds of things. He could command attention when he walked into a room.

Lizzie had always loved that quality in a man.

She frowned as she continued to watch.

What an ugly scene. Lizzie could understand how people wanted to preserve the area, especially because it was best for these horses. But she knew that other people also valued progress. They didn't necessarily have evil intentions. Some might classify them as greedy, but that didn't mean they were.

Either way, it seemed like such a shame for this to be happening here in Cape Corral.

"Look, there's another wild horse!" Preston pointed to a chestnut-colored mare in the distance.

The horse seemed to be wandering about, almost as if clueless to the tension on the island. What Lizzie wouldn't give to feel a touch of that cluelessness. Instead, her problems—and the problems of others—constantly remained at the forefront of her mind.

She couldn't forget that she had some big decisions to make. She needed to set aside her own feelings, her own hopes and dreams, and do whatever was best for Preston.

Right now, her first priority was keeping him alive.

Pressure mounted on her shoulders. If only there was a clear-cut path to do so. But there wasn't.

As Lizzie mulled over the thoughts, a sound sliced through the air.

Her muscles went rigid.

The crowd seemed to hear the noise at the same

time. Screams emerged. People scattered. Ran for their lives.

That had been a gunshot, she realized.

Lizzie threw herself over Preston and hunkered down in the truck.

Dear Lord, what is happening? Please, keep my son safe.

CHAPTER THIRTY-ONE

DASH'S GAZE swerved to his truck when he heard the gunfire.

He looked over in time to see Lizzie and Preston duck low in their seats.

They were okay.

For now.

But the relief he felt was short-lived.

Another bullet pierced the air. The crowd had dispersed, running for shelter. As they did, Dash ducked behind a Jeep and drew his weapon.

He surveyed the area, trying to find the gunman's location.

The shooter appeared to be behind the sand dune.

Dash glanced to his left and saw Levi and Grant

poised for action behind other vehicles.

Most of the crowd had found safety.

But the situation was still dangerous.

Another bullet flew toward them, penetrating the side of the Jeep Dash used for cover.

This guy was shooting at Dash, wasn't he?

Dash would have to think about the why later.

Right now, he needed to concentrate on keeping everyone safe.

He and his team waited several minutes.

But no more bullets came.

Levi motioned for Dash to go right while he went left. Grant would remain on guard here.

Wasting no time, Dash remained low and headed toward the dunes.

This man was brazen. Pulling a gun in broad daylight showed guts—but not the kind of guts that Dash admired.

Dash crested the sand dune in time to see a motorboat speeding away in the distance.

Quickly, he pulled out his phone and put a call in to the Coast Guard. With any luck, one of their patrols would be able to find this guy.

But, for now, there was no way to catch him.

They needed to collect evidence and check on everybody who had been on the scene.

LIZZIE SHIVERED as she stood on the sandy road with Preston. Everything that was happening still felt surreal.

Had someone really just pulled out a gun and shot into the crowd? Why would they do that? What did they hope to prove?

She wanted to ask Dash all those questions. But she couldn't. Not right now.

He'd hurried back to check on them. But as soon as he saw they were okay, he needed to return to the crowd.

Lizzie looked across the way and saw Dash interviewing various people who'd been on the scene. Grant collected bullets and took pictures. Levi was on the phone.

What a nightmare.

Lizzie wasn't sure if she was the only one who'd noticed, but that gunman seemed to be aiming right for Dash.

Had it been Nicolai?

The man obviously knew how to shoot. He'd been in the military. He'd had guns at his home. From what Lizzie understood, the shooter had escaped in a boat.

Nicolai had been an avid boater back in the day. In fact, in high school he'd worked as a dockhand at a marina on Long Island.

As all the facts collided in her head, her unease continued to churn.

"Mom, I want to go home." Preston tugged on her arm.

"Back to New York?"

He shook his head. "Back to Dash's place."

Lizzie frowned. "You know that's not home, right?"

"I feel safe there. Especially when I'm with Goliath."

Lizzie slowly nodded, glad the boy had found comfort here. But she wasn't sure when they'd be able to leave this scene.

They went back to sit in Dash's truck to bide the rest of their time until they could leave the scene. When she'd been crouched over Preston during the gunfire, she saw a piece of paper on the floor.

As she sat in the driver's seat now, she spotted it again and tugged it from beneath the floor mat.

Her eyes widened at what she read.

It appeared that she wasn't the only one keeping secrets.

Dash had a few more of his own.

CHAPTER THIRTY-TWO

DASH TOOK Lizzie and Preston to the station. Someone would be here while Preston did schoolwork and while Lizzie worked on her computer. Time was of the essence right now as his team searched for this shooter.

Things had already been ugly today, but that outcome could have been a lot worse. Thankfully, nobody had been hurt when that gunman started firing.

But Dash couldn't stop thinking about the possibility that the man who'd been shooting was Nicolai. And, if so, he'd been aiming at Dash.

Why did this man, who was possibly obsessed with Lizzie, feel the need to take Dash out? Did he see Dash as a threat?

The questions left Dash feeling unsettled.

The Coast Guard had searched the waters for the shooter's boat, but they hadn't found it yet. They hadn't given up, but Dash knew the chances they'd locate it were becoming slimmer and slimmer.

In the meantime, they would send the bullets out for ballistics, but Dash knew the results would take time. He wasn't sure, in the end, that the report would help them identify the shooter, but it might.

Meanwhile, none of the witnesses they'd talked to had seen anything.

For that matter, no one had recognized the picture of Nicolai that Dash had been showing people around town the past several days.

If this man was on the island, he was doing a fantastic job hiding.

In some ways, Dash didn't even see how that was possible.

Either way, pressure mounted on his shoulders with every passing moment. They needed to find this guy. Because now not only were Lizzie and Preston in danger, but this man was putting other people in this town in danger as well.

And that wasn't okay.

The day passed in somewhat of a blur. Mrs. Minnie stopped by the station and brought everyone some battered fish and fries for lunch, along with some coleslaw and cherry pie.

Finally, at six o'clock, Dash knew it was time to head back to his house for the day.

The ride back was quiet, but Dash sensed that Lizzie had things she wanted to ask him.

As soon as they were inside with the doors locked, she turned to him. "Can we talk?"

"Of course." Dash glanced at Preston. "Hey, P-man. Would you mind taking Goliath upstairs and tossing the ball down the hallway?"

"You don't want me to take him outside?" Preston squinted in confusion.

In other circumstances, Dash would have said yes. But he couldn't risk the two of them being outside right now, not with everything that had happened. "I think the hallway will work out great. It's getting chilly outside."

Preston shrugged and grabbed the orange ball from the floor. He called for Goliath, and the two of them trotted upstairs.

Then Dash turned to Lizzie and waited for whatever it was she had to say.

LIZZIE LICKED HER LIPS, uncertain how to start. Yet she didn't feel she could keep this to herself, even if it wasn't any of her business.

"You're the one who's been buying property here on the island, aren't you?" she finally blurted.

Dash's face lost its color, and he rubbed his neck. "Why would you think that?"

"I saw a paper in your truck. Plus, I can tell you're keeping secrets. Your gaze shifts whenever somebody talks about the property that's being bought up. I just didn't put it together until today. Am I right?"

He remained silent for a moment, and Lizzie wasn't sure he was going to answer. Maybe she'd been off-base, but she didn't think so.

Finally, Dash nodded. "You're right. I'm the one who's been buying up some of the land."

"Why would you do that? Are you seeing this as an investment opportunity?"

He shook his head, his eyes widening with alarm. "No, it's not like that at all. I'm buying the land because I want to conserve it."

Realization swept through Lizzie. Had she understood him correctly? "So you don't want to build?"

"No, not at all. I love this island the way it is. I'm buying that land so the Fergusons can't."

Lizzie almost wanted to laugh. Here she thought she had Dash all wrong. Yet she didn't. Dash was *exactly* who she thought he was—a true cowboy. Despite their relationship issues, he was still a good guy.

"Why would you keep that a secret?" That was the one thing that didn't make sense to her.

Dash shrugged. "I don't want people to change their perception of me. If I start telling folks, then they're going to look at me in a different way. I don't want that. I like being an . . . an everyman here."

She could admire his stance but there were still some details that didn't make sense to her. "I understand that you want to keep your wealth a secret, but how are people going to feel when they find out about this?"

"I've put all the proper barricades in place so they shouldn't be able to find out. I have an LLC set up that's hard to trace back to me. But that doesn't mean—"

Lizzie waited for whatever else he was about to say.

"But that doesn't mean what?"

Dash looked away and rubbed his jaw. "That doesn't mean that no one will find out."

"No, it doesn't."

Dash's gaze locked with hers. "Somebody here knows. I've been getting calls and threats. My lawyer has been getting threats as well."

What? Someone had taken things that far? She didn't like the sound of that. "Do you think it's the Fergusons?"

"I think that, even if it is the Fergusons, they're too smart to let it be traced back to them. But if somebody thinks that sending me nasty emails is going to get me to change my mind . . . they're wrong."

Lizzie's mind continued to race. "Do you think that shooter today was somebody who knows what you're doing?"

Dash rubbed his neck again before shaking his head. "I don't think so, Lizzie. This person who knows what I'm doing . . . they're more the type to take legal action. Honestly, I suspect the shooting today had something to do with you. Of course, we're still investigating."

She shook her head, trying to process their conversation. It felt nice to focus on Dash for a change, even if the subject was sobering. A better picture of the man in front of her was coming together in her mind.

"I think it's great what you're doing, Dash," she finally said. "I just don't want it to come back to bite you in the bum."

"Believe me, I tried to think all the details through. This was the best solution that I could come up with. I want to protect this island. But I also want to protect myself from the scrutiny that comes with having money."

Just as Dash said the words, a loud knock sounded at the door.

Dash bristled beside her.

Who could be here at this time of night?

Lizzie braced herself for a replay of yesterday—a replay of the bullets piercing the wood.

Because she knew this was far from over.

Had trouble shown up again?

CHAPTER THIRTY-THREE

DASH MOTIONED for Lizzie to go into the kitchen. When she was safe, he peered out the window.

He braced himself to see a gunman. To hear gunfire. To feel pain.

Instead, he spotted Levi standing at his front door.

Dash released the breath he held before striding to the door and opening it.

But as soon as he saw his friend's red face, he knew that something was wrong.

Levi stared at Dash and shook his head in disbelief. "You're the one who's been buying up properties on Cape Corral?"

Dash ran a hand through his hair. This wasn't the way his friend was supposed to find out.

"It's not what you think," Dash started.

Levi's hands went to his hips. "I can't believe you. I can't believe you would keep this from us."

"I can explain—"

Levi sliced a hand through the air, all his passion bubbling to the surface. "I don't want to hear any explanations."

"How did you even find out?" Dash had been so careful.

Levi shook his head, his jaw still hard and his eyes angry. "The Fergusons told me. Gloated about it, for that matter."

Dash rubbed his neck. He shouldn't be surprised. "The only reason they told you is because they want to divide us."

"I don't care what their motivations are. I expect shenanigans like this from them. I don't expect secrets from you."

Dash knew he needed to explain himself soon before everything crashed around him. "Levi, you need to hear me out."

"Just answer me this—is it true? Have you been buying lots here on the island?"

Dash sighed, wishing Levi would realize it wasn't that simple. Finally, he nodded. "I have been."

Levi stared at him another moment before

shaking his head, his gaze still unyielding. "You're not the person I thought you were."

"Levi—"

Without saying anything else, Levi turned on his heel and stormed away.

Dash took a step, about to go after him.

Then he changed his mind.

He'd let his friend cool down. Then they would talk when they were both more level-headed.

But it looked like the life that Dash had carefully constructed here in Cape Corral was quickly eroding, much like the sand dunes after a storm.

He closed the door and looked back at Lizzie. She stood near the couch, an almost sympathetic look in her gaze.

Dash didn't even know what to say. Besides, he didn't owe Lizzie any more explanations. She'd probably be leaving this island before too long.

He'd told himself from the start that he shouldn't get too close. His initial thoughts had been correct. He should have listened to his gut instinct instead of his heart.

Right now, there was nothing else to talk about. Everything was on the line, and failure wasn't an option.

LIZZIE SENSED that Dash needed some time by himself. So she'd gathered Preston, and they escaped to the bedroom where they were staying. Preston sat on one bed reading a book while she lay in the other bed trying to catch up on some emails she'd gotten behind on.

But her mind wasn't on work.

It was on anything but work, actually.

She could understand, on one hand, why Dash had kept the fact that he'd been purchasing land a secret. Wealth *could* change the way people viewed you.

Money made some people want to be your friend, and it caused others to judge you.

Still, Dash probably should have trusted his friends enough to tell them what he'd been doing. As soon as Lizzie realized the truth, she'd feared that something like this might happen.

Part of her wanted to go downstairs, to be with Dash in his moment of struggle.

But he'd made it clear her comfort wasn't welcome, and Lizzie needed to respect that boundary.

Despite that resolve, something about Dash was

still so very tempting. She'd never met anybody like him. When he smiled, everything felt right in the world. When she saw him with Preston, Lizzie could easily envision a future with this man.

But those dreams were dangerous.

She needed to stay away from thoughts like that. They'd only end in heartache.

Someone lightly knocked on her door.

She assumed Dash had brought Goliath. He'd promised he'd bring the dog up before he went to bed.

Lizzie put her computer down and rushed to answer.

When she saw Dash's face as he stood on the other side of the door, she knew something was wrong. She stepped into the hallway so she wouldn't alarm Preston.

"What's going on?" she asked.

"I put out a search for Nicolai after you told me about him," Dash started, his voice low. "I just heard back about it."

Her throat tightened with anticipation. "And?"

"And the police found his body last week up in New York. He's dead."

CHAPTER THIRTY-FOUR

DASH WATCHED the emotions roll over Lizzie's face.

She glanced back at Preston through the crack in the door. "I'll be right back, honey. Okay?"

"Okay, Mom." The boy slumped down farther in bed, his eyes drooping. He would be asleep soon.

Once Lizzie closed the door, she turned to Dash. Questions filled her eyes. "Are you sure Nicolai is dead?"

Dash nodded, halfway wishing he had different news for her. At least with Nicolai, they had a suspect. Now, they had no one. "Officials have positively identified this man as Nicolai."

Her hand covered her mouth as she stared up at

Dash. "That's the last thing I expected to hear. How did he die?"

Dash softened his voice, knowing not everyone was used to receiving news like this. He needed to be sensitive yet make the urgency of the situation clear. "Apparently, he was shot and left in a ditch."

Lizzie gasped. As Dash saw the emotions washing over her, he reached for Lizzie. Despite his reservations, he sensed she needed someone to lean on right now.

He wrapped his arms around her. "I'm sorry, Lizzie."

She shook her head, still stiff as if in shock. "I just can't believe this. I can't believe Nicolai is dead. It's not that I cared for him, but I didn't wish harm on him either."

"I understand."

"And if he's dead . . . then who's behind these things that have been happening here?" Fear stretched through her voice.

That thought had been echoing in his mind also. "That's a great question. You don't have any other ideas? There aren't any other people who were giving you a hard time?"

Lizzie stepped back, and her eyes raced back and

forth with thought as she seemed to consider his question. "Not really. I mean, no one obvious."

"Maybe we need to consider people who aren't obvious then."

She ran a hand through her hair, a far-off look still in her gaze. She didn't say anything for a moment until finally, "I'm going to think about it. I don't really know. I don't know what to think right now."

She was obviously dealing with a lot right now, and Dash wouldn't push her. "I know this is a lot for you to comprehend. Even though Nicolai is dead, someone is still out there. We have to figure out who it is."

Lizzie nodded slowly, something close to resignation fluttering through her gaze. "I guess this explains why nobody on the island has seen Nicolai."

"That makes sense now." He'd thought the same thing.

"I guess so." Her gaze fluttered up to meet his. "Thank you for letting me know."

Dash nodded and reluctantly let go of her. Instantly, he missed Lizzie's warmth. Her scent. Her.

He just missed her.

But this was for the best, he reminded himself.

For more than one reason.

Why weren't his emotions getting that memo?

COULD NICOLAI REALLY BE DEAD?

As Lizzie lay in bed, the question continued to turn over in her mind.

That didn't even seem like a possibility.

If Nicolai wasn't behind the events happening here, then who was? Who would have this much hatred toward her?

Lizzie searched her thoughts, trying to come up with someone.

Could someone be angry because of her company? She *had* fired an employee about a month ago for stealing several clothing items. The woman's husband had been upset, of course. But would he take things this far?

One of Lizzie's neighbors had also gotten angry a few months ago when Lizzie had refused to cut down a tree. The leaves from it had been falling in his yard, and he didn't want to rake them. She'd apologized but refused to cut down the two hundred-year-old oak. Could Mr. Billings really be so upset with her that he'd followed her here and gone through all this trouble?

Lizzie seriously doubted either of those people were behind this. Those little tiffs shouldn't have set off a firestorm.

Her thoughts continued to turn over.

Maybe if Lizzie could find the man she'd paid to bring her to the island by boat, he would have some information. Maybe someone had come to him and asked him questions about her. That could have led to someone finding Lizzie here.

Or maybe she should track down the person she'd sold her car to at the harbor. Even though everything was done through a cash transaction, could someone have gained information about her whereabouts that way?

The only other possibility of where this person had discovered information about her was the management company. Lizzie had to put her credit card on file in order to stay at the house. But the rental agent had promised not to run her card. Could that be the way Lizzie's hideout had been discovered?

Who would have gone through all that trouble just to locate her here? It would have to be someone either desperate to find her or full of absolute contempt.

Lizzie didn't like the sound of either of those things.

Dear Lord, what am I going to do?

She closed her eyes, wishing she could sleep. But she knew that was an impossibility. She had to figure out who was behind these dangerous incidents, not only for her sake, but for Preston's . . . and for this town's.

CHAPTER THIRTY-FIVE

AS THE SUN rose across the Atlantic, he stood at the edge of the woods and watched Lizzie, Preston, and Dash inside the house.

They looked like a family, though they weren't.

None of them had taken his hints yet. What did he have to do to scare them out into the open? Every time he looked, Lizzie was within arm's reach of her son.

That would never work.

He needed a way to separate them.

And he was becoming desperate.

Today, he would follow them again.

His window of opportunity to make a move was becoming narrower. He didn't have all the time in the world to do this. Not by any stretch of the imagination.

Why didn't anyone realize this?

He'd never expected it to be this hard.

But he wasn't one to give up either.

He'd find the opportunity he was looking for.

He glanced beside him in the woods as he saw something move.

A smile curled his lips.

A snake.

As he watched the creature slithering away, an idea formed in his head.

He just might have a plan after all.

But all the pieces had to fall into place.

The timing had to be right.

If he correctly predicted what was going to happen next, then he would win. But there were still several things that needed to happen.

His smile widened.

Maybe today would be his day.

Because time was running out.

In more ways than one.

CHAPTER THIRTY-SIX

DASH FELT the tension in the air as he walked into the Community Safety building the next day, Lizzie and Preston at his side.

Though he hoped to smooth things over, it didn't look like that would be happening.

As soon as he'd arrived, Levi had left to do patrol. Grant wasn't scheduled to come in but would take his shift tonight. Dillon and Colby were both busy checking equipment and were effectively avoiding him. No doubt they'd already heard the news.

It looked like Dash would have to wait until later to explain himself.

"Do you guys want to help feed the horses?" Dash asked. "Or if you need to get right to work, I understand."

"Yes! Can we, Mom? Can we?" Preston stared up at his mom.

"Of course."

He led them into the stable and pulled out some hay. As he taught Preston how to feed the horses, the boy was full of questions.

"Where did Shadrach live before, when the fire broke out?"

"In the mountains of Virginia."

"Is he happy since he came here?"

Dash nodded. "I think so. It took some adjustment. He was a bit of a fish out of water at first. But now he's one of the finest horses we have here on the island."

"Do you think I could ride him sometime?"

Dash glanced at Lizzie, who mostly stood in the back and watched them work. "If it's okay with your mom, then it's okay with me."

"Can I, Mom?" Preston turned to her.

"I don't see why not. As long as Dash is okay with it."

At least Dash had given the boy something to look forward to during these otherwise grim times.

Dash still had no leads on who might be behind these threats toward Lizzie or the gunfire that had happened yesterday. If Nicolai was dead . . . then they were back at square one.

Dash also had no idea how he was going to make things better between him and his coworkers.

He understood why they didn't want to talk to him right now. They were still processing and wrestling with their assumptions. Dash only wished they'd assumed the best of him, but he could see where the situation was sticky. He just needed to give them some space, and then he could clear things up.

He hoped.

As soon as he went back into his office, he planned on looking into a few people Lizzie had given him names for.

Dash just needed a break in this case. Just one. Just something that would give them a clue as to where to look next.

Because Dash knew in his gut that this guy wasn't going to stop.

He shuddered to think what that meant.

HE WAS a bit of a fish out of water at first. But now he's one of the finest horses we have on the island.

Dash's words stayed with Lizzie.

She never thought she'd relate to a horse. Yet she felt at the moment like she and Shadrach had something in common.

They'd both come to the island having faced tragedy. Would Lizzie be like Shadrach? Would she rise to the challenges around her?

Or was she meant to return to the life she'd left behind?

She wasn't sure.

Lizzie looked up from her desk when she realized that Preston had been gone longer than he said he'd be. He'd run down the hallway to get a snack from the vending machine. It wasn't the food choice of champions. But they were in a bind, so it would work for now.

She stood and stretched, her eyes blurry from working on the computer. She could use a break to stretch anyway. Too much desk work exhausted her.

As she stepped into the hallway, she saw it was empty. No Preston. Not only did she not see him, she didn't hear him either.

Strange.

Lizzie paced toward the back of the building where the vending machines were located, fully expecting to see Preston still mulling over his choices. Peanut butter crackers or cheese puffs. The decision was always hard, especially for an eight-year-old.

When Lizzie reached the machines, no one was there.

The first surge of apprehension shot up her spine.

Where was Preston?

She let out a little laugh as a realization hit her.

Most likely, her boy had tracked Dash down and was talking his ear off. Lizzie just needed to find Dash, and then she'd find her son. Preston had put the man on a pedestal and seemed to constantly seek him out.

Lizzie continued down the hallway, glancing through each doorway as she passed, just to be certain she hadn't missed Preston.

When she reached Dash's office, she saw the cowboy sitting there looking at some papers.

Alone.

Another trickle of worry went down her spine.

"Hey, Dash," she started. "Have you seen Preston?"

He looked up and shook his head. "I thought he was with you."

"He was, but he went to get a snack. He's been

gone for a while, so I decided to check on him. He's not at the vending machines."

Dash rose from his desk. "I'll help you look for him."

Lizzie's muscles tightened as they walked down the hall together. There was probably a logical explanation for this.

But the last time she'd assumed that, Lizzie had found Preston in Wash Woods staring down a wild boar.

"I searched every room in the building, but Preston was nowhere to be found." Lizzie's throat clogged at the words.

Dash lightly touched her arm, zapping her back to reality and away from her worst-case thoughts.

"We're going to find him," he murmured.

But as quickly as her worry slipped away, the emotion returned with a vengeance—hurtling closer to panic with every passing minute. What if this man who'd been taunting them had somehow slipped into the building? What if he'd grabbed Preston?

"I don't know where he could be." She rubbed her throat, hardly able to get the words out.

Suddenly, light filled Dash's gaze. "I bet Preston is with the horses."

Dash was probably right. But Lizzie wasn't sure

that thought comforted her. Preston had no business going outside by himself. Not with everything that had been going on.

They jogged toward the back of the building and then outside to the stable. Just as they stepped inside, Lizzie spotted Shadrach.

The horse stood out of his stall, the sunlight behind him illuminating his strong silhouette.

She sucked in a breath.

Preston sat atop him, attempting to ride him . . . alone.

"Preston!" Lizzie yelled. What was he thinking?

Her son glanced back at her, a triumphant expression on his face.

"Look what I did, Mom! All by myself!"

But the triumphant look didn't last long.

Just then, a snake slithered toward them.

Shadrach rose up on his back legs and let out a startled neigh. His nostrils flared as panic lifted his legs again.

As he did, Preston went flying into the wall behind him.

CHAPTER THIRTY-SEVEN

"PRESTON!" Lizzie rushed toward her son, praying he was okay.

Please, don't let him be hurt. Please, Lord!

As she darted across the stable, Dash ran toward Shadrach. He had to get the animal under control before he trampled the boy.

Tears rushed to Lizzie's eyes as she nearly collapsed on the ground in front of her son. He groaned and opened his eyes, his gaze not fully focused on her.

"Mom?" he asked in a small voice.

She ran her hand across his cheek to wipe away the tears. "I'm here, sweetie. I'm here."

Behind her, Dash had led Shadrach away. Now, it

sounded like he was on the phone calling for backup.

Lizzie wanted to pull her son into her arms. But she knew better than to move him. What if Preston had injured his neck? She couldn't risk that.

But the thought made a cry stick in her throat.

Preston could have been killed.

She should have put aside her work for the day. She should have suggested they play games together. Do something.

Instead, this had happened.

"Where's that man?" Preston whispered, his voice almost a moan and barely discernable.

"What man?" Lizzie had no idea what her son was talking about. Was he seeing things?

"Before I saw you . . . there was a man . . . at the other end of the stable. He had a . . . snake."

Lizzie and Dash exchanged a look.

Had the man who'd been hunting Lizzie left that snake? Was he trying to hurt Preston? Or was her son seeing things?

Her head pounded harder.

Dash peered outside before quickly returning to her and Preston. "I don't see anyone. Do you think he's delirious?"

Lizzie sucked on her bottom lip before shaking her head. "No, I don't think so."

Just then, Levi rushed into the stable, along with Colby and Dillon—both of whom were firefighters and brought their medical equipment.

They surrounded Preston to examine him.

As they did, Dash tugged Lizzie back to give them space to work. She folded her arms across her chest, wishing she'd been the one hurt and not her son.

A cry shook her body. As it did, Dash slipped his arm around her, and Lizzie buried her face in his chest.

What if her son wasn't okay?

She could hardly bear to ask that question.

DASH SQUEEZED Lizzie's knee as they sat at the island clinic, waiting for word from the doctor.

They'd stepped out of Preston's room while Dr. Knightly examined the boy. The rooms were small, and the doctor and nurse indicated they needed space.

Lizzie hated to leave her son, but Dash assured her that Preston was in good hands.

The woman looked beside herself after what had happened. Dash couldn't blame her. What happened in the stable had been scary. But the outcome could have been much worse.

The two of them hadn't had a chance to talk since the incident, but they needed to.

Dash cleared his throat, knowing this might be too soon. But he also knew that time was of the essence in situations like this.

He had told Levi what Preston had said, and he knew his colleague was searching the area around the stable for footprints or any other clues to prove someone had been out there. But Dash needed to get Lizzie's take on the whole thing.

"Do you really think Preston saw someone?" Dash quietly asked.

She shrugged and wiped her red-rimmed eyes again. "Preston looked pretty convinced."

"He did." Dash couldn't argue with that.

"But the only reason someone would have done that was . . ." She pressed her lips together, almost as if she couldn't finish the sentence.

"If they wanted to put you in this situation," Dash finished. "Someone could have known how much horses don't like snakes and tried to spook Shadrach."

Lizzie turned toward him, her gaze full of questions. "But how did someone even know Preston would be out there?"

"Maybe someone lured him out," Dash suggested "Or, more likely, someone was watching and waiting for the right opportunity. It's hard to say."

"Why would anyone want to hurt a sweet little boy?" Lizzie's voice broke, and she looked away, as if facing reality was too big a burden to bear.

Dash rested his hand on her back, his heart panging with empathy. "I don't know. I wish I could tell you. I wish I could take this whole experience away. But I can't."

Lizzie wiped beneath her eyes again. "I know you can't. I just . . . I just feel so lost right now."

Dash opened his mouth then shut it again. There was no right thing to say.

But there was only one thing he *wanted* to say.

But was this a good time?

He licked his lips. "Don't go, Lizzie. Stay here. Let us help you."

She stared at him a moment, something brewing in her gaze—something intense. "Why would you want me to stay here, Dash?"

He swallowed hard, considering what to say.

Part of him wanted to declare his feelings.

But another part remained cautious.

Lizzie let out a sigh and shook her head. "You know what? Never mind. Just please—don't be so sweet to me only to push me away. It's like you're trying to break my heart or something."

She'd totally misinterpreted Dash's silence. "Lizzie, I would never—"

Before he could finish his statement, Dr. Knightly appeared in the doorway.

Lizzie stood, her full attention on the doctor. "How's Preston?"

Dash held his breath as he waited to hear an update.

CHAPTER THIRTY-EIGHT

DASH COULDN'T STOP THINKING about what Lizzie had said.

Her words made sense.

With one hand, Dash pulled her closer, and, with the other, he pushed her away.

It wasn't fair to her.

Lizzie wasn't like all the past women that he had dated.

No matter what kind of hints Preston had given about her, that didn't mean the words were true or that they hadn't been misinterpreted.

Judging people's motives was a tricky venture.

Asking somebody if she just wanted to be together because of his money wasn't exactly couth. Usually, people's intentions were proven through the test of time—proven by watching someone's actions and reactions.

And, so far, Lizzie had shown no ill intentions. She'd never asked Dash for anything. Even when he tried to give her things, she always hesitated before accepting. Throughout everything, she'd been grateful for his help.

He'd been stupid, and Dash should have never pushed her away.

Images of Isabell flooded his mind more often than he wanted. The woman had really done a number on his heart. Now it seemed like anyone Dash dated in her aftermath would pay the price.

Except that wasn't the way this was going to work. Dash wasn't going to let Isabell have that kind of control in his life anymore.

He glanced at Lizzie. She leaned over Preston as the boy rested in his bed. Two hours had passed since Dr. Knightly had given her the good news that Preston was okay. He had a slight concussion, but nothing was broken. He should be just fine.

Lizzie had so much love and affection for her son.

Dash couldn't tell her everything on his mind right now. But he would tell her how he was feeling soon. When the time was right.

Before it was too late.

He'd meant what he said when he promised to keep her safe. He'd never forgive himself if something happened to her or Preston on his watch.

Too much had already happened.

Dash glanced at his watch. It was already 9:00 p.m. Visiting hours were over—except Lizzie could stay with her son, of course. Dash was only allowed to stay because he was law enforcement.

He hated to leave her alone at a time like this—and he wouldn't, as long as he was welcome here. Lizzie hadn't pushed him away yet.

Lizzie kissed Preston's forehead again before stepping toward Dash. "I think I'm going to go get some water. Now that I know he's okay, I realize I'm feeling lightheaded."

"You want me to grab some for you?"

She shook her head. "I need to stretch my legs a moment."

"I can walk with you."

She glanced back at Preston and frowned. "I don't want to leave him alone."

Dash peered into Preston's room again and saw the boy's eyes were closed. When Dash glanced back, a familiar figure appeared in the hallway.

Dash waved him over.

"Hey, Colby, can you stand here by Preston's door while we get some water?"

Colby sauntered toward him. "Of course. Whatever I can do to help. I just brought someone in for a jellyfish sting. Another exciting night here in Cape Corral."

"Sounds like it," Dash said. "We'll be right back."

Colby didn't bother to go inside Preston's room. Instead, he leaned against the doorway outside and propped a leg up against the wall.

Dash started to put his hand on Lizzie's back to lead her toward the vending area.

But he thought better of it.

Instead, he stuffed his hand into his pocket and walked beside her down the hallway.

LIZZIE WAS SO thankful that Preston was okay. Things could have turned out so much differently.

For the second time since they had arrived here in Cape Corral, Preston could have been killed.

If Lizzie counted the bullets that had been shot through the front door at Dash's house, that would make three times—and the protest would be four.

Lizzie couldn't fathom what was going on.

Whenever she tried, her head started to pound. None of this made sense.

That man who had been following her at home had to be Nicolai.

But Nicolai was dead.

Who had killed him? And why?

But questions didn't comfort her. Not at all.

She started to reach into her pocket to grab some change when Dash put some coins in the vending machine for her. "Go ahead. My treat."

"You don't have to do that."

"But I want to."

She wasn't in the mood to argue. Instead, she punched in the numbers for her selection and, a moment later, a water bottle dropped to the bottom of the vending machine. Lizzie picked it up, unscrewed the cap, and took a long sip.

She hadn't realized just how exhausted she was from the emotional day. Even though she could use some sleep, there was no way Lizzie would leave Preston here by himself tonight.

To her son's credit, he *had* already charmed the doctor and the nurses. In fact, one of the nurses had taken to calling Preston her favorite patient ever. Preston ate up all the attention.

Lizzie fought a smile at the thought of their

interactions. She needed to look for whatever good she could in this otherwise horrible situation.

"What are you thinking?" Dash leaned closer and studied her face.

She glanced up at him, realizing how close he was standing. Despite that, she didn't step back. "Do you really want to know?"

"Of course I do."

"To be honest, I'm wondering why such a good boy has to go through all of this," she blurted. "It doesn't seem fair."

The corner of Dash's lip flickered down in a frown. "Life definitely isn't fair sometimes. That's for sure. I understand that a little too well."

Lizzie took another sip of water, her throat dry and achy. "He's a strong boy. Losing my sister was a tragedy. But being able to raise Preston? It's been a privilege. A blessing. Every single sacrifice I had to make was worth it."

"You're a good mom, Lizzie. He's lucky to have you."

Warmth stung her eyes. "I don't feel like a good mom. I feel like all of this is my fault."

"Lizzie . . ."

As Dash reached for her, she raised a hand. The last thing she needed was to add confusion about their relationship on top of the stress she already felt.

Quietly, they walked back down the hall toward his room.

But as they turned the corner, Lizzie spotted Colby slouched on the floor.

Almost like he'd passed out.

Lizzie dropped her water bottle and sprinted toward Preston's room.

Something was wrong.

She felt it in her gut.

CHAPTER THIRTY-NINE

DASH DARTED into Preston's room.

As he feared, the bed was empty.

As Lizzie let out a cry, Dash rushed toward Colby and patted his cheek. The man's eyes startled open, and his gaze darted around.

"What happened, Colby?" Dash demanded. "Where's Preston?"

He let out a groan before instantly alerting. "One minute, I was standing here, and, the next minute, something came down on my head. Then everything went black."

"Did you see anything?" Dash rushed, urgency in every syllable.

Colby shook his head before flinching again. "No. I'm sorry."

Dash and Lizzie exchanged a glance before sprinting down the hallway. They had to find Preston. Wherever he'd gone, it couldn't be far away.

Dash barely paused as he reached the front desk. "Have you seen Preston?"

The nurse's eyes widened. "I did. His . . . father checked him out. He had the paperwork and everything. He said his wife was coming in a moment, after she gathered their son's things. I just—"

Dash felt the tension between his shoulders pull tighter. His father? This person they were dealing with had thought everything through, hadn't he?

"Where did they go?" he asked.

The nurse pointed to the front door. "They just left, probably not even three minutes ago."

Three minutes could seem like forever in a situation like this.

Dash told the nurse she needed to check on Colby. Then he and Lizzie took off toward his Bronco. As they climbed inside, he handed Lizzie his phone.

"Call Levi," Dash ordered as he cranked the engine. "You need to tell him what's going on. We need to have everybody out here looking for Preston."

"Dash . . ." Lizzie's voice wavered.

Despite his promise to himself that he wouldn't touch Lizzie anymore, Dash reached over and squeezed her hand. "It's going to be okay. But you need to make that call. Now."

Lizzie looked at him for only one more second before nodding and finding Levi's number on his phone.

As she did that, Dash took off, scanning the landscape around him.

No one could get off this island without a boat.

It was that fact and that fact alone that gave Dash any hope.

WITH EVERY SECOND THAT PASSED, Lizzie's anxiety grew.

Who was this man who'd taken Preston? Where could they have gone?

Though she knew the police were searching all over the island, that knowledge hardly brought her any comfort. They'd even organized search teams of volunteers to look for her son, but her gut told her they would do no good.

An hour had passed, and Preston was nowhere to be found.

It was like he'd disappeared from the face of the earth.

Lizzie's head spun. Her lungs tightened. Worry electrified her thoughts.

This couldn't be happening.

But it was.

Finally, Dash stopped in front of the Community Safety building, which served as Ground Zero for their search efforts.

Dash turned to Lizzie, some of the hope fading from his eyes also. He didn't have to tell her that. Lizzie could see it. Could sense it.

"We're going to find him," he assured her.

Lizzie squeezed the skin between her eyes. "I wish I believed that."

"That man can't get off this island," Dash said. "We have the Coast Guard as well as the marine police looking for any boats in the water. We've alerted authorities on the mainland too, and they're standing guard at the harbors and docks there. We're utilizing every resource possible to find Preston."

She forced herself to nod, though the motion felt robotic. "I know. I appreciate everything you're doing. I really do. But I should have never left Preston's side . . ."

Dash squeezed her shoulder. "I'm sorry this

happened. The truth is, even if you had been there, there's a good chance this person would have knocked you out too."

"He's *my* responsibility! This is my fault!" Tears burst from Lizzie's eyes.

Dash slipped his arm around her and pulled her closer. She started to pull away again but didn't. She craved human touch right now. Craved comfort, reassurance.

"I'm sorry, Lizzie," he murmured.

"We have to find him," she muttered into his chest.

"Maybe it would be better if you stayed here."

She swung her head back and forth, a new surge of energy bursting through her. "There's no way I'm going to sit still. I want to be out there looking for Preston. I *have* to find him."

"Okay," Dash said. "We'll keep looking. Let me just head inside real quick and see if there are any updates. But I'll look with you as long as you want me to. Okay?"

She pulled away from him, her red-rimmed eyes lined with appreciation. "Thank you. Thank you."

CHAPTER FORTY

THREE HOURS LATER, they still had no answers.

Where could that man have taken Preston? Dash wondered. It made no sense. This island wasn't that big. Though it would be an exaggeration to say they'd searched every inch of it, that was how it felt.

Levi had pulled out a map of the island and spread it over a table in the conference room. Levi, Grant, and Dash looked over it now, marking off quadrants that needed to be searched again.

Dash was thankful his colleagues were taking this seriously.

As they should. An abduction was serious, whether you knew the people involved or not.

Things like this just weren't supposed to happen here on Cape Corral.

Lizzie stood beside Dash as they waited for Levi's instructions. With every passing moment, she seemed more and more frail.

Dash knew that she was a strong woman. But something like this could break even the most courageous person.

"We're going to divide into search groups, and we're going to go door to door until we have answers," Levi finally said. "I'm going to divide everybody into eight groups and assign each group a different quadrant from this map. We're going to search every crevice in each of those quadrants until we find this boy."

"Any word from the Coast Guard?" Dillon, the fire chief, asked.

Levi shook his head. "Not yet. They're still patrolling the waters. There are white caps out there tonight, so not very many people have boats out. In some ways, that's making their search a little easier. As soon as they hear something, they'll let me know."

Dash squeezed Lizzie's elbow again as he felt her shudder.

He couldn't even begin to imagine what was going through her mind right now.

As Grant began to divide volunteers into groups,

Levi strode across the room toward Lizzie. His expression was both no-nonsense and compassionate.

"I think you should stay here," Levi told her.

Lizzie sucked in a breath. "But I want to be out there—"

"I know." His voice remained calm and even. "But when we find Preston, we're going to need you here. It's important that you're one of the first people your son sees."

Her eyes widened before she squeezed them shut again. With resignation, she finally nodded. "I guess that makes sense. I just hate not doing anything."

"You're doing plenty. Right now, I just need you to hang in for a little bit longer."

"I understand." Lizzie nodded again, more slowly this time. "Thank you for everything that you've been doing."

Levi patted her shoulder. "You've got this whole town behind you right now, Lizzie. We're searching, and we're praying. We're going to find Preston."

With that reassurance, Levi walked away.

Dash started to pull Lizzie toward him again.

He didn't want to do the whole push her away and pull her closer thing again. He hoped that's not what Lizzie thought. Because all Dash could think about was how she needed someone to be strong for her.

And he wanted to be that person.

LIZZIE ALTERNATED BETWEEN PACING, drinking coffee, and praying as she passed time at the Community Safety building.

Levi and Dash's words made sense. She should be here when they found Preston.

If they found him.

She shook her head. No, she couldn't think like that. They were *going* to find him. She just needed to be patient.

But where could her son be? Why had this man taken him?

She tried to shut out the worst-case scenarios that continued pounding her thoughts. Dwelling on those wouldn't do her any good right now, and Lizzie knew that.

Time seemed to crawl around her. Even though she knew everybody was doing everything they could, nothing moved fast enough for her taste right now.

She wanted Preston to be back with her.

She wanted him to be here now.

She sighed and leaned against the wall, feeling another wave of lightheadedness. She had to keep herself together right now. There was no other choice.

What would Amanda think if she knew what was happening?

She wouldn't be happy. Lizzie had promised to take care of her little boy. Lizzie felt at this moment like she'd failed miserably.

Oh, Amanda. I'm so sorry. I don't know what I was thinking. Maybe every decision I've made has been a bad one. I thought I was doing my best. I really did.

But Lizzie knew that wasn't what her sister would think. Her little sister had thought Lizzie hung the moon.

Lizzie often thought about her sister. Lizzie suspected that Amanda had begun dating someone from her high school. It wasn't until she was seven months pregnant that their family realized she was pregnant. Amanda had covered her baby bump by wearing large sweatshirts and baggy clothing.

When they'd tried to find out who the father was, Amanda had refused to tell them.

It never made sense to Lizzie why Amanda had

kept the father's name quiet. She'd only said that he wanted nothing to do with their baby, that he'd already left town, and that he wouldn't be coming back.

Lizzie hadn't understood it. But every time she tried to ask questions, her sister only clammed up even more. Lizzie finally realized that the best thing she could do was just to offer to help Amanda out at a time like this. Her interrogation was doing no good.

There were times now when she wished she'd asked more questions.

Back then, she'd assumed Amanda would tell her more later, after time had passed.

But that chance hadn't come. Amanda had suffered from extreme bleeding that the doctors hadn't been able to stop in time after she gave birth.

Lizzie looked up as somebody ran into the building holding something in his hands. "Look what I just found!"

Lizzie recognized the man. It was Mr. Henderson, the person she'd bought her truck from.

In his hands, he held a flannel shirt.

Just like the one Preston had been wearing when she'd taken him to the hospital.

CHAPTER FORTY-ONE

THREE MEMBERS of the Nags Head canine team had come into Cape Corral to help search for Preston. They'd arrived just in time. The crew was now searching the area near Wash Woods, in the area where Preston's shirt was found, trying to follow the boy's scent.

Part of Dash wanted to head out there himself. But Levi said he needed him here helping with logistics. That was just as well since the other part of Dash wanted to stay close to Lizzie.

Dash looked over and saw Lizzie talking to Dani, Levi's girlfriend. Seeing that she was occupied at the moment, Dash strode toward Levi. His boss stood near the operations table, marking areas off on the map.

Dash paused in front of the table. "Maybe we should get a copter out there looking for Preston."

Levi's gaze flickered toward him before focusing on the map again. "That would be a great idea, but we'd have to have something like that approved by the town council before we could pay for it."

Dash rubbed his neck, hesitating for just a second before saying, "I could pay for it."

Levi jerked his gaze toward Dash before narrowing his eyes. "I suppose you could, couldn't you?"

Dash let out a long breath and rubbed his neck as he contemplated his next words. "Look, I know this isn't the best time to talk about this. But I didn't want people to think I was some rich guy who rode into town trying to save the day."

"Would that have been all that bad?" A healthy dose of skepticism stained Levi's voice.

"When you're constantly judged for how much money you have, then, yes, it can be."

Levi shook his head and marked off another area on the map. "But we're all your friends, Dash. It should be different with us."

"I didn't think it would matter who was buying up the land, as long as the land was being preserved. That seemed like the important thing.

Besides, how am I supposed to bring up a subject like that? Was I supposed to say: *Hey guys, guess what? I bought five hundred acres here on Cape Corral. Just thought you'd want to know.* It would have seemed pompous."

Levi glanced at him again, and his shoulders softened some. "Maybe you're right."

"I'm still the same Dash you hired three years ago. I still love this island, and I only want the best for it."

Levi offered a slow nod. "I'm thankful that it's someone like you who's buying up this land instead of the Fergusons—especially if you're not planning on building."

"Of course I don't want to build." Dash lowered his voice. "I don't know how, but the Fergusons somehow found out it was me, and they're not happy."

Levi's eyes narrowed. "Any idea how they found out?"

Dash had been trying to figure that out. "I don't know. But I have a feeling they're the ones who've been trying to buy me out. When that didn't work, they sent some pretty ominous messages."

"Threats?" Levi raised an eyebrow.

Dash remembered the messages he'd received

and frowned. "Probably subtle enough not to count as a threat. They're too smart for that."

Levi frowned again. "Good to know. I'll keep that in mind. Because I'm still determined to preserve this place. But, right now, we need to find Preston."

Dash stepped back and nodded, happy that he'd been able to get this out in the open. He didn't want the tension between them to somehow hurt their search efforts. They needed to be able to trust each other.

There were still talks that needed to be had, but this would do for now.

"How about I call about that copter?" Dash said.

Levi nodded. "That would be great."

"WHEN DO you think we'll hear something?" Lizzie paced over to the operations table, where Levi and Dash stood.

How much longer could she wait? It felt like hours had passed, even though it was mostly minutes.

Still.

This was the worst kind of torture she'd ever felt in her entire life. Not knowing where her son was made her feel crazy. Not being able to protect her son when he needed her made her want to die inside.

Levi frowned and released a long breath. "Unfortunately, the dogs lost the scent. They're trying to pick it up again. We just need to give them some time."

Lizzie's shoulders drooped. That wasn't what she wanted to hear.

"The good news is that we're going to bring a copter out." Levi glanced at Dash, the two exchanging some kind of silent message. "We're going to search the island from the air."

"Why do I feel like there's a but in there?" She held her breath as she waited for his response.

"The only problem is that the woods are so thick, it's going to be hard to see through the canopy," Dash explained. "Still, it's worth a shot. We need to give this everything that we can."

Lizzie nodded. "Of course. And if the copter doesn't work? And the dogs?"

Levi grimaced but the look quickly disappeared, replaced by a professional, non-emotional expression. "We'll still keep searching by foot. We're not going to give up, Lizzie. I promise you that."

She nodded, though she felt tattered inside.

This wasn't the way things were supposed to work.

Up until a year ago, things had been going so well in her life. Her business had never done better. She'd been able to socialize more as Preston got older. She'd even met Nicolai, which seemed like a positive thing at the time.

Then, quickly, everything had fallen apart.

Including her.

Lizzie felt like she was barely keeping herself together right now.

She looked up as she felt Dash's gaze on her. He studied her, that worried expression still present on his face.

She quickly looked away before he saw too many of her thoughts.

For someone who didn't want to get that close to her, he was certainly concerned and attentive. A big confusing mess, if you asked her.

Either you liked someone or you didn't.

But Lizzie just couldn't figure Dash out.

Either way, she had bigger concerns to deal with at the moment.

Levi's phone rang, and he stepped away to answer.

Lizzie waited, hoping this might be some kind of

update. She wasn't leaving the spot until she found out.

A moment later, Levi returned with a grim look on his face.

"That was a call from up in New York," he started. "From the detective who's working the case of Nicolai Rossi."

"Did they discover something?" Her heart pounded in her ears as she waited to hear what he'd learned.

"They have a suspect for his murder."

"Who?" Lizzie didn't bother with pleasantries.

Levi probably wasn't allowed to say. But she wanted to know anyway.

"They think someone named Stephen Hodge is responsible," Levi said. "Does that name ring any bells?"

Her heart pounded in her ears. The name did sound familiar.

But why?

Where had she heard that name before?

She had to remember. Preston's life might depend on it.

CHAPTER FORTY-TWO

LEVI, Dash, and Lizzie all sat around Levi's computer, trying to find out everything they could about this Stephen guy. Dash hoped something they learned might lead them to answers.

With every second that passed, Preston was most likely farther and farther away.

That wasn't okay.

"It looks like he went to high school up in Pennsylvania." Dash pointed to the computer screen.

Lizzie's back straightened. "Was it Hickory Ridge High School?"

"It was." Levi glanced at her. "How did you know that?"

Lizzie didn't answer the question. "When did he graduate?"

Levi rattled off the year.

As soon as he did, Lizzie's head drooped toward her lap, almost as if she was defeated. "I think I know who he is."

"Who is it, Lizzie?" Dash turned to her, intent on getting her to focus right now.

She lifted her head and drew in a deep breath, as if composing herself. "I can't say this with any certainty, but that man graduated from my high school a couple of years before I did."

Realization spread through Dash. Of course . . . "You think this is Preston's father, don't you?"

"It's the only thing that makes sense. Maybe this guy has been determined to try to get Preston back this whole time. It would explain his obsession . . ."

"But he never tried to contact you?" Dash asked. "Seems like a more logical step. If he fought hard enough, he'd probably be able to get some type of paternal rights."

Terror shot through Lizzie's gaze at the statement. "I can't even think about that. My sister never said much about Preston's dad, but I had the impression he wasn't everything she hoped he would be. When he found out that Amanda was pregnant, he didn't want anything to do with the baby. Honestly, part of me thinks Amanda was relieved when he left."

Levi frowned and leaned back into his chair. "Still, this seems like a lot of trouble to go through just to get his son."

Lizzie shook her head and folded her arms over her chest as if chilly. "I don't know what to say. This whole time I thought it was Nicolai. This is going to take a moment to process."

"If Nicolai was intent on winning you back, maybe he saw this Stephen guy hanging around and confronted him," Dash suggested.

Lizzie nodded. "That makes sense. I can totally see that happening."

"But now we need to figure out how to find him." Dash stared at the man's image on the screen.

No doubt this guy would be a tough opponent. He was six foot five inches tall and had muscles built like a professional wrestler. But the look in his eyes confirmed Dash's fears.

The man just looked mean, like someone without a soul.

Lizzie's phone rang, and she nearly jumped out of her seat at the noise.

Quickly, she pulled the device from her pocket and glanced at it. Her panicked gaze met his then

Levi's. "I don't recognize the number. Should I answer?"

"Answer and put it on speaker," Levi instructed.

Her hands trembled as she did as Levi said.

Dash resisted the urge to reach over to help steady her. Finally, she rested her arms on the desk, and they waited to hear who was on the line.

———

"I HAVE PRESTON," a deep voice said.

Lizzie could hardly breathe when she heard the man's ominous tone. "What do you want? I'll do anything to get him back."

"I need you to meet us. *Alone.*"

Lizzie gripped the phone harder. "Just tell me where."

"I mean it," the man growled. "If you come with somebody else, it's not going to end well. For any of you."

"Mom!" Preston yelled in the background.

As Lizzie heard the terror in her son's voice, her blood froze.

She'd meant her earlier words. Whatever this man wanted, Lizzie would be willing to give him if it meant getting her son back.

She glanced at Dash and Levi, waiting for any instructions. Levi jotted something on a piece of paper.

Keep him talking.

Levi and Dash were probably trying to trace the call, she realized.

She nodded and swallowed hard. "Can I speak to him? To Preston?"

"He's fine," the man barked. "You're going to have to trust me on that one."

"Why did you take him?" Her voice trembled. "Where are you?"

"You're asking too many questions. I need you to meet me in thirty minutes. I'm going to text you the address. But I mean what I said. If you get law enforcement involved, you're not going to like the outcome."

"I understand." She glanced at Dash again, watching for his confirmation. He gave her a nod to let her know she was doing fine. "Send me the address. I'll be there."

Before she could say anything else, the line went dead.

Lizzie nearly dropped the phone onto the desk. Her hands wouldn't stop trembling, no matter what she did. This all seemed surreal, like a nightmare.

But at least she'd heard Preston's voice.

"What's going to happen once I meet him?" Her gaze flickered up to Levi and Dash. "I doubt this man is going to just hand Preston over."

She had no idea what this man's end goal was.

"We need to figure out a plan," Levi said. "The man wasn't on the phone long enough for us to trace him and get a head start."

That's what she'd figured.

Her gaze locked on Dash's. "All I know is that I want my son back. I'll do whatever it takes to get him."

CHAPTER FORTY-THREE

LIZZIE FIDGETED in her truck again.

The address had been texted to her, just as he'd said.

In a whirlwind, she'd donned a bullet-proof vest beneath her shirt. Been wired. Been instructed.

Then she'd taken off.

She only had twenty minutes left to get there, after all. She didn't want to take any chances.

Then she'd driven toward the GPS location the man had sent her. Dash crouched on the floor beside her, out of sight from anyone watching but near enough to help.

Levi and his guys would remain close—but not close enough to give away their location.

This whole thing felt risky. Too risky.

But Lizzie would do anything—anything!—to get Preston.

Still, questions swirled in her head.

She just couldn't figure out this guy's game plan.

If he wanted Preston, why hadn't he used other means to get the boy? Why hadn't he tried to do it legally?

Though Lizzie was glad the man had called her, what good would it do for her to meet him? How did she fit into the plan?

She glanced at her phone again and sighed. "Why haven't I gotten another text yet?"

It was fifteen minutes past the time they were supposed to meet. Where was this guy? Did he know Dash was here? Had he changed his mind?

"Give him time," Dash whispered. "He wants to make sure you know that he's in control of this and not you."

Maybe that made sense. But it didn't make her feel any better.

Moments of silence passed until finally Lizzie cleared her throat. The timing couldn't be worse, but in some ways that made this easier to talk about. Her wire wasn't on yet, so no one else could hear her.

"Why did you push me away?" she asked quietly.

She slouched in the seat so no one would see her lips moving.

Dash nearly did a double take at her, almost as if he hadn't understood her question. "That? Oh, Lizzie . . ."

"I want to know."

He let out a breath. "Mostly, it goes back to someone I dated. Her name is Isabell. I thought we were in love and that we would get married. But then I discovered that she was only with me because of my money. She never cared about me at all. That realization was really hard to stomach."

Had Lizzie just heard him correctly? "So you thought that I was a gold digger?"

He shrugged in the darkness. "Not at first. But then Preston told me about how important image is to you. And that you thought money was a big deal and—"

Lizzie couldn't listen to this anymore. She let out a harsh cynical laugh. "I can't believe this. I'm in fashion. I have to care about image!"

Dash let out a sigh and ran a hand over his face. "Honestly? This whole thing is a struggle that I deal with—not knowing if people like me for me or if they like me for my money. But that night before we kissed . . . I thought I saw something in your eyes change. I thought you might have recognized me."

"Dash . . ." Lizzie released the breath she held. "I don't want your money."

"Honestly, my gut has been telling me that all along. But once bitten, twice shy, as the saying goes."

She shook her head. "No, you don't understand. I don't want your money or *need* your money. I'm doing well on my own."

Dash paused for a moment before shrugging. "What do you mean?"

She leaned her head back and let out another long breath. "Dash, I run my own online clothing boutique. It's called Lizzie Rae. It's grown beyond anything I could have ever imagined, and . . . I can take care of myself."

"You own Lizzie Rae?" Recognition stretched through his voice.

Surprise washed through her as she glanced at him. "You've heard of it?"

"My cousin *loves* that clothing line. She's always on the app buying new things."

"That app was one of the more innovative things I was able to do," Lizzie said. "I figured out how to make technology really work for the business. There's so little overhead because of this. I don't have to pay for storefronts or an overabundance of employees. Everything is done online."

Dash stared at her, his eyes narrowing. "That means you also run the blog . . . Bizzie Lizzie."

She nodded. So Dash had heard of that too? Wasn't he full of surprises?

"I decided I wanted to share what I've learned about being a business owner and entrepreneur with other people who were just getting started," she said. "So I began that blog in hopes of helping people. Again, just as with the boutique, I never expected it to become as popular as it did."

"You were named one of the top 100 business-women in the US by *Newsweek* magazine." Dash shook his head. "I didn't recognize you from the article, but I remember reading about your business."

"That's right. I was."

Dash let out a harsh chuckle and shook his head. "I can't believe this."

"I know what it's like for people to like you because they want something from you. It's not fun. But it's not fun being unfairly judged either."

"Oh, Lizzie . . . I'm so sorry."

Just then, her phone buzzed.

It was a message.

From the man who'd taken Preston.

Walk north through the woods 300 feet. I'll be in touch.

———

THE LAST THING Dash wanted was to send Lizzie out into Wash Woods alone. But if he went with her, the man who'd grabbed Preston was sure to notice. The perp might harm her or Preston.

He knew they couldn't risk that.

Still, someone had to protect Lizzie.

She glanced down at him as he crouched on the floor. "If I don't come back from this . . ."

Grief clutched Dash's heart at the thought of that. "Don't talk like that. You're going to come back."

"But if I don't, thank you for everything that you've done. You've been a real lifesaver." Lizzie started to reach for the door handle when Dash grabbed her hand.

"I mean it, Lizzie," he told her. "You're going to make it through this. Then you and I are going to have a long talk. Promise me that."

She pressed her lips together, as if holding back the emotions glimmering in her eyes. "I wish I could promise you that. But I have no idea what's going to happen tonight."

At her words, Dash knew what he had to do.

He'd already donned an all-black outfit. He'd blend in out there, and he knew the area well enough that he could maneuver through the terrain better than most.

Most likely, better than this man who'd taken Preston.

Dash only knew they didn't have time to waste.

Not only were Wash Woods dangerous, but so was the man who'd grabbed Preston.

So much wasn't on their side right now.

Dash prayed that God surrounded them with an army of angels to guard their every move.

CHAPTER FORTY-FOUR

LIZZIE COULD HARDLY BREATHE AS she wandered through the woods. The trees felt like they reached out to grab her. At any moment, she expected the sand to disappear from beneath her, making her a prisoner to this forest. She waited to be confronted by a wild animal—another boar or a snake.

But she would face all those terrors if it meant getting Preston back.

In her gut, she knew that this was too easy. There was more to this story. More that would play out here tonight.

Just what was this guy's game plan?

A tremble spread from her core all the way to her fingertips.

She wouldn't do anything to ruin this. Yet she couldn't deny the anxiety she felt.

Dear Lord, please help me. Watch over me. Protect Preston above all.

Lizzie may not have given birth to Preston, but he was hers. She knew that without a doubt. She couldn't love a child more than she did him.

She shoved a branch out of the way as she continued deeper into the dark wilderness.

Could she see herself in Cape Corral long term?

It felt like a real possibility. Maybe she would think about the opportunity more when this craziness was over.

If this craziness ever did end.

A cry lodged in her throat at the thought.

What if this didn't end the way she'd hoped?

No, she couldn't think like that. She *had* to stay positive.

Finally, Lizzie paused in the woods. Three hundred feet.

She had to have arrived.

As a breeze rushed over her, she almost wished she could keep walking. At least, when she was moving, she could concentrate on something other than the sounds of the forest around her. Something other than the snapping of branches and the leaves as they scratched together.

She pressed her hands together, trying to ward away a chill that began deep inside her.

What now? Was the man here? Was he watching her?

Lizzie's throat tightened as she glanced around, looking for any signs of life.

It was too dark. She couldn't see anything except cryptic branches and a thick, fortress-like wall of maritime forest. The sand would mask the sounds of anyone coming.

She liked this less and less all the time.

As her phone buzzed, she nearly jumped out of her skin.

At least, Lizzie still had service out here.

In this very spot she did, at least. She knew reception could be temperamental out here.

She glanced down at her screen and read the words there.

Go deeper. Walk north until I tell you to stop.

DASH WAS careful to remain quiet as he crept through the woods. He'd always been nimble on his feet, and he prayed that today would be no different.

Remaining in the shadows, he trailed Lizzie.

She didn't know he was there. He hoped the man who had Preston didn't know that either. But Dash had to be careful.

For all he knew, this guy could be hiding nearby. The last thing Dash needed to do was to stumble upon him. He *had* to be careful.

Preston's life depended on it.

So did Lizzie's.

The bad feeling in Dash's gut grew with every step he took.

He had no idea how this would turn out. Had no idea what this man's game plan was. Had no idea what to expect.

Dash *did* find comfort in knowing that Levi and Grant, along with the backup officers from Nags Head, were also waiting just out of sight.

They had to plan each move very carefully in order to assure that nothing backfired.

But Dash knew enough to realize there was no assurance of that.

Anything could happen out here.

He paused behind a tree and glanced out.

Lizzie had stopped walking. She stared at a small opening on a patch of sand in the middle of the woods as gnarled trees curled their branches around her.

Even from where he stood, Dash saw her shudder. Just enough light came from the waning gibbous moon to make that out.

He'd do anything to take Lizzie's place right now. To try to take some of this burden from her.

He couldn't do that.

But when this was all over, Dash prayed that he could make things right.

As he stood there, he listened. Watched.

He didn't see anybody else around.

Where was this man?

Where was Preston?

Finally, he heard Lizzie's phone buzz. She glanced at it before moving through the woods again.

Again? Just how far would she go into this wilderness? Every step deeper she went only made the risk greater.

But that man probably knew this.

Just as before, Dash continued following.

When Lizzie stopped again, he glanced around, trying to get his bearings.

The Jezebel Tree.

The notorious tree already had so many stories surrounding it.

Mostly, they were about a seductress who'd been found hanging from its branches more than a century ago. As the folklore went, no one knew if someone had killed her or if she'd taken her own life.

Those who were superstitious liked to say she still haunted this area.

Dash clearly spotted the tree in the distance.

This was where everything had begun. The place where Dash had saved Preston from that wild boar and where he had met Lizzie for the first time.

What would tonight hold for them?

As Dash stood there, he saw a man step out from the other side of the woods, Preston in tow.

He sucked in a breath and braced himself for whatever would happen next.

CHAPTER FORTY-FIVE

"PRESTON!" Lizzie's heart leapt into her throat as she reached toward the boy.

"Oh, no," the man grumbled, tugging the boy back. "Don't even think about coming any closer."

Lizzie's gaze fell on the gun the man held. The weapon wasn't pointed at Preston, but it was clearly there, clearly a threat.

Lizzie froze, her gaze swerving from the weapon back to Preston.

Her son appeared okay. No signs of injury were visible. His gaze remained defiant.

She fought a smile at the sight of it. Lizzie always knew Preston's stubbornness would serve him well one day. This situation just might be that time.

But a lot could still go wrong.

Lizzie's gaze flickered up to the man.

Stephen Hodge.

Just as they'd suspected.

Anger trickled through her fear.

How dare this man show back up in their lives like this? He'd had a chance to be a father to Preston. Had a chance to make a life with Amanda.

He hadn't been interested.

"What do you want?" Her voice cracked as she stared at him.

Stephen glowered down at her, his meaty figure puffed up as if to maximize intimidation. "You're going to need to come with me."

"Why would I do that?"

"Because the three of us should be together."

"The three of us?" Lizzie asked. "I don't understand."

He shook his head. "I started with different intentions. I started watching you because I needed you to sign some papers."

"What kind of papers?" Lizzie's voice sounded thin, even to her own ears.

"Papers giving me permission to use Preston's blood."

Nausea swirled in her gut. "Why are you doing this . . . Stephen? Why do you need his blood?"

Lizzie decided to play that card, to let him know that she knew his identity. It gave her a small amount of control in the situation.

His gaze darkened. "How did you know my name?"

"I put the pieces together." She glanced at Preston again, wishing she could shield him from this conversation. But she couldn't. Not right now. "Why are you back in my son's life now after all of these years?"

"That's not important. I just need you to come with me. I promise you. We'll be happy together. We all will be."

"Where would we even go? We're in the middle of the woods." A chill washed over Lizzie as she felt eyes watching them. A wild animal? Or were the guys with the forestry division out here?

She had no idea.

"You don't worry about that," Stephen said. "You just come. If everybody listens and cooperates, then nobody else will be hurt."

Lizzie drew herself up to full height. "You mean, like you hurt Nicolai?"

The man grunted. "He wasn't supposed to see me. Then he had to go get all brave by confronting me. It was his own fault. He should have stayed out of it."

His words caused her breath to catch. This man had justified murder. What else would he justify?

She didn't want to know.

"I'm sure that whatever you want, we can deal with this in a rational manner," Lizzie said. "There's no need for all the dramatics right now."

"You have no idea what you're talking about." His voice swooped lower.

"Then why don't you tell me? Because I've been trying to figure things out."

Something cracked in the distance, and all three of them tensed.

A moment later, a tiny critter scampered from branch to branch.

Lizzie let out the breath she held.

At least it wasn't a boar.

Not yet.

"We don't have time to talk now," Stephen said. "I have a boat waiting to take us away from here. The three of us . . . we can start again. It's how it should have been. How it should be."

A boat? The Coast Guard was out on the water.

That's what Dash had said. Certainly, officials would see Lizzie and Preston. Maybe this would end.

Could that really be possible?

But there were also a lot of things that could go wrong. There were white caps out there. It was dark.

Or what if this man somehow made it to the mainland. What would he do with them?

"I know what you're thinking," Stephen said. "But the captain I hired is an expert at covert operations. He can navigate these waters without any light. But that means we need to move before that sun starts to come up."

A sick feeling churned harder in Lizzie's gut. This man sounded confident that this was all going to work out in his favor.

What if it did?

Lizzie didn't want to ask herself that question.

But she had no choice.

DASH LISTENED FROM BEHIND A TREE.

Sure enough, Stephen Hodge stood there.

What exactly did this man want? That was what Dash couldn't figure out.

But Dash feared if Lizzie and Preston got on that boat that Dash would never see them alive again.

This man would get whatever it was that he wanted from Lizzie, and then he'd finish them off.

Dash had no doubt about that.

He needed to think of a way to stop them without getting anyone hurt.

The situation was precarious, at best. Deadly, at worst.

Dash wiped his neck as an insect landed there.

They were so isolated out here in Wash Woods. He wished he could quietly ask Levi what he and his guys were doing. But he couldn't do that without drawing attention to himself.

So Dash remained quiet. It was a risk he couldn't take.

"I don't want to go anywhere," Preston announced, stomping his foot.

If the situation had been different, Dash might have smiled at the boy's feistiness. Dash only hoped right now that the boy's stubbornness didn't get anybody hurt.

"Stop acting like a brat," Stephen muttered, his hand squeezed Preston's arm. "If I say we're going to go, we're going to go."

"You're not my dad!"

Stephen jerked the boy closer and leered down at him with an eerie smile. "Actually, yes, I am."

Anger burned through Dash's blood, and he fisted his hands at his sides. It took every ounce of his self-control to stop himself from rushing onto the scene. Why did Stephen have to pull the boy into this?

"I don't care what you say, you'll never be my dad." Preston's defiant gaze stared up at the man. "You know why? Because I don't like you. You're a bad person."

"Watch your mouth!" The man raised his hand as if he might slap the boy.

"No!" Lizzie lunged closer but stopped herself as the man raised his gun. Instead, her gaze turned to her son. "Preston, I need you to calm down. Okay?"

"But, Mom—"

"Not right now," she told him. "We're going to get through this. I need you to remain calm."

"Yeah, *Son*." Stephen said the words with disgust. "You'd be wise to listen to your mom. Or should I say your *aunt*?"

"You're not going to hurt him with those words." Lizzie's voice trembled, but an underlying confidence grounded her statement. "Preston knows the truth. I haven't withheld anything from him."

Stephen grunted, as if her declaration surprised him. He quickly recovered and grabbed Lizzie's arm.

"Come on," he ordered. "Let's go. There's no more time to waste. I've run out of patience."

CHAPTER FORTY-SIX

LIZZIE NEEDED TO THINK QUICKLY.

Stephen was becoming more and more unhinged by the moment.

She couldn't risk what might happen if he totally lost it.

"What changed?" she blurted, trying to buy a little more time. "You left us alone all this time. Why come back now?"

The man grunted as he glared at her. "I went to the doctor, that's what."

Realization settled over Lizzie at his words. "You need something only a blood relative can give, don't you?"

It was the only thing that made sense.

"That's right. Turns out I have a blood cancer

and need a transfusion—except I have a rare blood type that only .6 percent of the world has. In order to have the transfusion I need, I need someone who matches me. I need Preston."

"How do you know his blood type matches?"

"I was able to break into his doctor's office and find out."

Lizzie shook her head as she realized the desperation of it all. "Why didn't you just ask? Why go through all this trouble?"

Stephen snarled. "I knew you guys would never forgive me after what I'd done to Amanda. I knew that wasn't going to work. I'm not ready to die yet." His voice weakened, just for a moment before he squared his shoulders again.

"You could have tried us."

"If my dad finds out that I had a child out of wedlock, he'll write me out of his will. I'll lose *everything*. That's why I had to do this on the down low."

Lizzie sucked in a breath as more puzzle pieces clicked in place. "Now I can see why Amanda didn't want me to know who you were. I'm not sure why she ever fell for you."

"What can I say?" He shrugged, not bothering to hide his smugness. "I can be charming when I want to. But I get bored very easily. She should have never gotten pregnant, but she refused to take care of things. That's when I opted out. I offered Amanda money to terminate things, and she refused."

"That's because my mom wasn't a buffoon like you are," Preston blurted, his eyes narrowed with contempt.

Stephen scowled again. "Listen, how many times do I have to tell you, you little brat, you need to keep your mouth shut."

"So you killed Nicolai—" Lizzie said.

"He caught me watching you."

"And you followed us here."

"I lurked in the shadows. You were clueless."

"And when you got here?" Lizzie continued, trying to buy time.

"All I had to do was ask a few questions, and I was able to figure out where you were staying. Easy-peasy."

"You took pictures of us." Lizzie still tried to put all the pieces together.

"That was the strange thing. As I watched you, I realized that the three of us . . . we're meant to be together. This is my chance. I'm not sure how much longer I have. I want to make things right."

Cold, stark fear shot through her. "What do you mean?"

"I want the three of us to be a family. We belong together."

"But I thought you just said your dad can't find out?" The man wasn't making sense.

"He won't know who Preston really is. In fact, my father will think it's great that I took in a single mom and her child." He grinned. "It will all work in my favor."

"Stephen . . ."

"Lizzie, you're remarkable. I wasn't expecting to think this. But you are. So beautiful and kind." His gaze darkened. "You should have never been with that other man. He's not right for you."

"So you had to teach him a lesson?"

"He was supposed to answer the door that day. When that didn't work, I had to take more extreme measures. I don't have time to waste. Can't you understand that?"

Suddenly, Lizzie had an idea.

She wasn't sure if it would work.

But it might be worth the risk.

Because she knew that she and Preston could *not* go with this man.

As Preston started to argue with the man again, Lizzie lunged toward Stephen. Using every last ounce of her body weight and strength, she shoved him to the ground.

"What?" Stephen muttered a few profane words.

He started to reach for his gun that had fallen from his hand. But Lizzie kicked it out of the way before he could grab it.

"Once I get my hands on you," he growled.

As Stephen tried to stand up, he found he couldn't.

Because Lizzie had pushed him right into the pit of quicksand that had trapped her just a week earlier.

DASH SUCKED IN A BREATH.

Brilliant move, Lizzie. He was impressed, to say the least.

But he didn't have time to stand there and marvel over it for too long.

Instead, Dash darted from the shrubbery concealing him.

Lizzie gasped and turned around, almost as if expecting to see another wild animal.

Instead, her shoulders drooped with relief when she spotted Dash.

Dash wanted to pull Lizzie into his arms and tell her everything on his mind. To apologize profusely.

But he hoped he'd have time for that later.

Right now, Dash grabbed the gun Lizzie had kicked across the sand. Carefully, he tucked it into his waistband as he turned to Stephen.

The man clawed at the ground around him, trying to pull himself from the sandy pit that suctioned him in place.

There was no use.

Stephen wasn't getting out without a lot of help.

"This isn't over," the man growled. "Lizzie, don't do this to me. Give me a chance!"

Lizzie didn't bother to acknowledge him.

Preston dove into his mother's arms. The two of them clung to each other.

There had never been such a beautiful sight.

They were both okay.

"Police!" Levi, Grant, and the other officers appeared from the woods.

As they did, the sound of a helicopter hummed overhead, and a spotlight came down over the area. The Jezebel Tree came into view, as did Stephen, who struggled to pull himself from the quicksand.

As his colleagues took control of the scene, Dash stepped back.

It looked like this was really over.

Stephen would be arrested and stand trial for what he'd done. He would be going away for a long time for the murder of Nicolai Rossi as well as his other crimes.

If the man survived that long.

If what Stephen had said about his health condition was true, then he just might die a lonely death in prison.

As Levi and Grant apprehended the man, Dash strode to Lizzie.

When she looked into his eyes, there was no mistaking the gratitude there.

And the affection.

In one move, Dash pulled Lizzie and Preston into his arms.

"I'm so glad you're both okay," he muttered. "Good thinking back there, Lizzie."

"Who would have ever thought that our bout with the quicksand would have actually worked in our favor in the long run?" Lizzie let out a weak laugh.

Dash smiled and took a small step back. "Sometimes, things have a way of working out like that."

"Yes, they do." A smile fluttered across her face.

Dash leaned down to Preston's eye level and examined him quickly.

Just as he thought, the boy looked okay.

Stephen had to keep the boy healthy in order to use his blood.

"You hanging in?" Dash asked him.

"I'm fine." Preston raised his chin. "I knew you'd find me. And my mom too."

Dash admired the boy's confidence.

"Can you teach me how to ride a horse tomorrow?" Preston asked, almost as if nothing had happened. "I still want to learn."

Dash let out a chuckle. This boy didn't forget. His resilient attitude was certainly admirable. It would get him far one day.

"Come on," Dash said. "Let's get you guys out of these woods and somewhere a little more welcoming."

CHAPTER FORTY-SEVEN

THE NEXT DAY was a flurry of activities.

So much so that Lizzie hadn't had a moment alone to talk with Dash. There had been too many interviews, along with checkups at the clinic and a whole investigation to take up everyone's time.

She and Preston had grabbed a quick nap in the afternoon.

But it wasn't until 8:00 p.m. that Lizzie and Dash actually had a moment to themselves.

Preston had gone upstairs to turn in early.

Lizzie and Preston were going to stay at Dash's place one more night. Just until things calmed down and Lizzie was able to get her bearings again.

After that, she would look at finding a place of

her own here in Cape Corral. A real place. Not just a rental.

She'd realized that this was the kind of place she wanted to raise Preston. A place where people knew their names. Where neighbors looked out for each other. Where they could breathe fresh air and explore and learn.

It was different from the urban area where their current house was located.

After being here, Lizzie didn't care if she ever went back.

But first, she and Dash needed to talk.

Dash stepped into the living room as Lizzie came down the stairs from putting Preston to bed. He paused, cowboy boots still on and hat tilted back on his head.

No doubt about it, the man was gorgeous. On the inside and the outside.

Lizzie had never imagined herself dating a cowboy, but now it was all she could think about. Especially the cowboy in front of her with his leather-scented Back in the Saddle cologne and his smoldering smile. The fact he'd been willing to give up everything to pursue an admirable career was the icing on the cake.

She paced closer to him. "Thank you for everything you did back there. I couldn't have done any of that without you."

"But you did," Dash reminded her, his eyes twinkling with respect. "You were the one who realized that quicksand was there. You used it to your advantage. It's all the guys at the station are talking about. We've seen a lot, but that was a first."

"I figured the move was worth a shot. I knew that we couldn't go with Stephen anywhere or we'd never be seen again." Lizzie paused, her thoughts still racing through the details. "Were you able to catch the man who was going to give Stephen a boat ride across the water?"

"We did find him, but he was innocent in this. Stephen told the man he was having a medical emergency and needed to get back to the mainland ASAP. The man had no idea all the details of what was going on. At least, that's how it seemed."

"The man wasn't from Cape Corral?"

"No, he was from Virginia—he has a house close to the state line. He actually used to work in the military so he knew his way around these waters, even in the dark."

"I'm just happy it didn't come down to us getting on that boat." Lizzie shivered as she said the words.

Dash stepped closer and rubbed her arms. "Me too. Things were really sticky back there for a while."

"Yes, they were. I guess Stephen needed me to sign the paperwork for Preston in order for the transfusion to happen. He was convinced that we would have said no if he asked us."

"He was concerned about his father's money, it appears. And, in the process, it sounded like he fell in love with you."

Lizzie shivered again. "Or something like that."

"Of course, you are easy to fall in love with."

Lizzie felt her cheeks heat and let out a soft chuckle. "Is that right?"

Dash's warm gaze remained on her. "It is."

She raised a finger, trying to slow the conversation. "Before we get to that, I thought I'd let you know that I did some research while you were at the office. I discovered Stephen's dad owns a big financial firm. He's known for being very demanding, with very high standards. Stephen stood to gain millions if he met his father's approval. I'm still not sure why he had to go through all of the theatrics, though."

"Honestly, I don't think that he was in his right mind. He was just desperate. That's what happens when people face death."

"I suppose you're right." Lizzie shook her head. "Part of me feels sorry for him and the other part hopes he goes away for a long time . . ."

"We all do."

Lizzie shifted. "Not to change the subject, but I need to get these details out of the way before we talk about . . ."

Dash raised his eyebrows. "Us?"

"Yes, before we talk about us." Why did that thought almost make her feel giddy? She cleared her throat. "What about the land you bought? Any updates?"

"Not really," Dash said. "The texts I got weren't enough to qualify as threats, so I can't charge the Fergusons with any crimes. For now, we're just going to keep an eye on the situation."

"I hope it resolves for you. I know it must be stressful."

"I hope it resolves also."

Lizzie took a deep breath as she looked up at Dash.

The conversation they had was definitely important.

But there were other things they needed to talk about.

Things involving Lizzie and Dash.

Personal matters.

Where did she even start?

Before she could figure out where to start, Dash said, "Look, Lizzie, I feel like I need to explain myself to you. I shouldn't have been so quick to judge—"

"No, you shouldn't have been."

He rubbed his neck, his gaze pleading with her for understanding. "It's just hard for me to trust that people really want to be around me for who I am. I feel like people are only interested in what I can do for them. But I'm sorry that I didn't give you the chance."

"I suppose I kept some secrets from you too," Lizzie said. "Maybe in my own way, I understand. I don't like to talk about everything I've achieved because it's not what I want to define me."

Dash moved closer and gently pushed a hair behind her ear. "I get that. I guess what I really need to know is: will you give me another chance?"

Lizzie didn't even have to think about his request. She'd been hoping that's what he'd say. "Of course, I will. I was hoping you would ask."

A grin spread across his face. Slowly, Dash leaned toward her until their lips met.

Lizzie hoped that this would be the first of many occasions they had to spend together. Because, for the first time in her life, she felt she had truly found a place to call home. Dash was a protector—of this place, and of her and Preston.

She could see herself making a life here, away from the hustle and bustle of the city.

But, really, anywhere with Dash and Preston would feel like home.

~~~

Thank you so much for reading *Breakwater Protector*. If you enjoyed this book, I would love for you to leave a review! Reviews are a huge help for building momentum and helping ensure a series will continue.

Stay tuned for *Cape Corral Keeper* coming soon!

To keep up with all the latest news, sign up for my newsletter at: www.christybarritt.com.

COMING SOON: CAPE CORRAL KEEPER

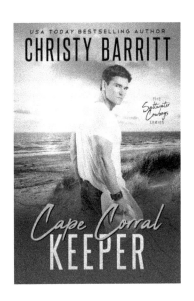

COMPLETE BOOK LIST

Squeaky Clean Mysteries:

#1 Hazardous Duty

#2 Suspicious Minds

#2.5 It Came Upon a Midnight Crime (novella)

#3 Organized Grime

#4 Dirty Deeds

#5 The Scum of All Fears

#6 To Love, Honor and Perish

#7 Mucky Streak

#8 Foul Play

#9 Broom & Gloom

#10 Dust and Obey

#11 Thrill Squeaker

#11.5 Swept Away (novella)

#12 Cunning Attractions

#13 Cold Case: Clean Getaway

#14 Cold Case: Clean Sweep

#15 Cold Case: Clean Break

#16 Cleans to an End (coming soon)

While You Were Sweeping, A Riley Thomas Spinoff

The Sierra Files:

#1 Pounced

#2 Hunted

#3 Pranced

#4 Rattled

The Gabby St. Claire Diaries (a Tween Mystery series):

The Curtain Call Caper

The Disappearing Dog Dilemma

The Bungled Bike Burglaries

The Worst Detective Ever

#1 Ready to Fumble

#2 Reign of Error

#3 Safety in Blunders

#4 Join the Flub

#5 Blooper Freak

#6 Flaw Abiding Citizen

#7 Gaffe Out Loud

#8 Joke and Dagger

#9 Wreck the Halls

#10 Glitch and Famous (coming soon)

Raven Remington

Relentless 1

Relentless 2 (coming soon)

Holly Anna Paladin Mysteries:

#1 Random Acts of Murder

#2 Random Acts of Deceit

#2.5 Random Acts of Scrooge

#3 Random Acts of Malice

#4 Random Acts of Greed

#5 Random Acts of Fraud

#6 Random Acts of Outrage

#7 Random Acts of Iniquity

Lantern Beach Mysteries

#1 Hidden Currents

#2 Flood Watch

#3 Storm Surge

#4 Dangerous Waters

#5 Perilous Riptide

#6 Deadly Undertow

Lantern Beach Romantic Suspense

Tides of Deception

Shadow of Intrigue

Storm of Doubt

Winds of Danger

Rains of Remorse

Torrents of Fear

Lantern Beach P.D.

On the Lookout

Attempt to Locate

First Degree Murder

Dead on Arrival

Plan of Action

Lantern Beach Escape

Afterglow (a novelette)

Lantern Beach Blackout

Dark Water

Safe Harbor

Ripple Effect

Rising Tide

Crime á la Mode

Deadman's Float

Milkshake Up

Bomb Pop Threat

Banana Split Personalities

The Sidekick's Survival Guide

The Art of Eavesdropping

The Perks of Meddling

The Exercise of Interfering

The Practice of Prying

The Skill of Snooping

The Craft of Being Covert

Saltwater Cowboys

Saltwater Cowboy

Breakwater Protector

Cape Corral Keeper (coming soon)

Seagrass Secrets (coming soon)

Carolina Moon Series

Home Before Dark

Gone By Dark

Wait Until Dark

Light the Dark

Taken By Dark

Suburban Sleuth Mysteries:

Death of the Couch Potato's Wife

Fog Lake Suspense:
Edge of Peril
Margin of Error
Brink of Danger
Line of Duty

Cape Thomas Series:
Dubiosity
Disillusioned
Distorted

Standalone Romantic Mystery:
The Good Girl

Suspense:
Imperfect
The Wrecking

Sweet Christmas Novella:
Home to Chestnut Grove

Standalone Romantic-Suspense:
Keeping Guard
The Last Target

Race Against Time

Ricochet

Key Witness

Lifeline

High-Stakes Holiday Reunion

Desperate Measures

Hidden Agenda

Mountain Hideaway

Dark Harbor

Shadow of Suspicion

The Baby Assignment

The Cradle Conspiracy

Trained to Defend

Mountain Survival (coming soon)

Nonfiction:

Characters in the Kitchen

Changed: True Stories of Finding God through Christian Music (out of print)

The Novel in Me: The Beginner's Guide to Writing and Publishing a Novel (out of print)

YOU ALSO MIGHT ENJOY . . .

LANTERN BEACH MYSTERIES

You can take the detective out of the investigation, but you can't take the investigator out of the detective. A notorious gang puts a bounty on Detective Cady Matthews's head after she takes down their leader, leaving her no choice but to hide until she can testify at trial. But her temporary home across the country on a remote North Carolina island isn't as peaceful as she initially thinks. Living under the new identity of Cassidy Livingston, she struggles to keep her investigative skills tucked away. When local police bungle their investigations, she can't resist stepping in. But Cassidy is supposed to be keeping a low profile. One wrong move could lead to both her discovery and her demise. Can she bring justice to the island . . . or will the hidden currents surrounding her pull her under for good?

Hidden Currents
Flood Watch
Storm Surge
Dangerous Waters
Perilous Riptide
Deadly Undertow

LANTERN BEACH PD

When Cassidy Chambers accepted the job as police chief on Lantern Beach, she knew the island had its secrets. But a suspicious death with potentially far-reaching implications will test all her skills—and threaten to reveal her true identity. Cassidy enlists the help of her husband, former Navy SEAL Ty Chambers. As they dig for answers, both uncover parts of their pasts that are best left buried. As facts materialize, danger on the island grows. Can Cassidy and Ty discover the truth about the shadowy crimes in their cozy community? Or has darkness permanently invaded their beloved Lantern Beach?

On the Lookout

Attempt to Locate

First Degree Murder

Dead on Arrival

Plan of Action

ABOUT THE AUTHOR

USA Today has called Christy Barritt's books "scary, funny, passionate, and quirky."

Christy writes both mystery and romantic suspense novels that are clean with underlying messages of faith. Her books have won the Daphne du Maurier Award for Excellence in Suspense and Mystery, have been twice nominated for the Romantic Times Reviewers' Choice Award, and have finaled for both a Carol Award and Foreword Magazine's Book of the Year.

She is married to her Prince Charming, a man who thinks she's hilarious—but only when she's not trying to be. Christy is a self-proclaimed klutz, an avid music lover who's known for spontaneously bursting into song, and a road trip aficionado.

When she's not working or spending time with her family, she enjoys singing, playing the guitar, and exploring small, unsuspecting towns where people have no idea how accident-prone she is.

Find Christy online at:
www.christybarritt.com
www.facebook.com/christybarritt
www.twitter.com/cbarritt

Sign up for Christy's newsletter to get information on all of her latest releases here: **www. christybarritt.com/newsletter-sign-up/**

If you enjoyed this book, please consider leaving a review.

Printed in the USA
CPSIA information can be obtained
at www.ICGtesting.com
LVHW011317060324
773597LV00016B/755